Remember This

S. T. Underdahl

flux
™
Woodbury, Minnesota

First Edition
First Printing, 2008

Book design by Steffani Sawyer
Cover design by Ellen Dahl
Back cover image © 2008 Digital Vision
Cover image of younger woman © 2008 by Rubberball/Punchstock
Cover image of older woman © Frank E. Kuhn

Flux, an imprint of Llewellyn Publications

Library of Congress Cataloging-in-Publication Data
Underdahl, S. T.
  Remember this / S. T. Underdahl.—1st ed.
    p. cm.
  ISBN-13: 978-0-7387-1401-1
  [1. Grandmothers—Fiction. 2. Alzheimer's disease—Fiction. 3. Best friends—Fiction. 4. Friendship—Fiction. 5. Dating (Social customs)—Fiction. 6. Family life—Fiction.] I. Title.
  PZ7.U413Re 2008
  [Fic]—dc22

                                                                2008013672

Flux
Llewellyn Publications
A Division of Llewellyn Worldwide, Ltd.
2143 Wooddale Drive, Dept. 978-0-7387-1401-1
Woodbury, Minnesota 55125-2989, U.S.A.
www.fluxnow.com

Printed in the United States of America

Acknowledgments

Heartfelt thanks to the people who make the magic happen at Flux: Andrew Karre for his invaluable input at every level of this project, Sandy Sullivan for her eagle eye, Steffani Sawyer for her amazing work on the postcard concept, Ellen Dahl for the wonderful cover, Courtney Huber for the back cover copy, and publicist Brian Ferry who takes the ball and runs with it.

Extra-special thanks to Tonja Rystad, my dear friend and my own personal "second set of eyes." Love and appreciation to my ever-supportive husband, Shane, and to the most inspiring ones of all: Navy, Fiona, Beck, Alexa, Chloe, and Jaiden.

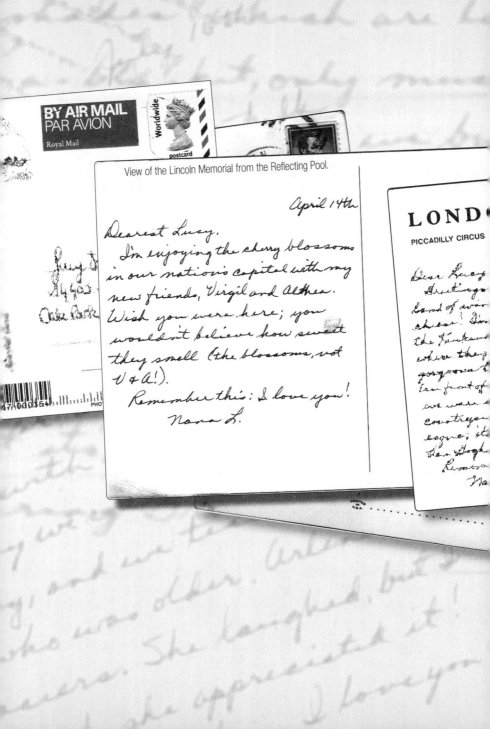

BY AIR MAIL
PAR AVION
Royal Mail

Worldwide
postcard

View of the Lincoln Memorial from the Reflecting Pool.

April 14th

Dearest Lucy,
    I'm enjoying the cherry blossoms
in our nation's capital with my
new friends, Virgil and Althea.
Wish you were here; you
wouldn't believe how sweet
they smell (the blossoms, not
V & A!).
    Remember this: I love you!
        Nana L.

LOND
PICCADILLY CIRCUS

one

Remember this: I love you. It was the special saying my Nana Lucy and I had for each other, ever since I was tiny. And it was the way Nana closed all the postcards and letters she sent to me on her travels over the years. But we never anticipated the significance those words would take on the summer after I turned sixteen—when Nana Lucy unexpectedly came to live with us.

As that summer began, I wasn't thinking about any of these kinds of things. I was busy with my best friend Sukie and our plans for the future. It was Sukie who came up with the "Sukie Hollister and Lucy Kellogg Self-Improvement Project," but I agreed to enlist immediately. It wasn't that we were unpopular or anything; we had plenty of acquaintances from school, and I don't think either of our names would have made an appearance on anyone's most-hated list. And yet, after two years of languishing in the land of quasi-nobodies at Williston High School, Sukie, at least, wanted more. And once I thought about it, I did too.

"I think we should try out for cheerleading," Sukie proposed on a Sunday afternoon in March. We were lying on the floor in her room, studying for the next day's chemistry test. "It'd be a great way to get our faces out there and meet a bunch of new people."

I looked up doubtfully from the equation I was trying to solve. "Yeah, but ... *cheerleading?* Not everyone likes cheerleaders." Personally, I'd been thinking more along the lines of signing up for the school newspaper staff, or maybe trying out for the golf team. Cheerleading wasn't the kind of popularity I'd necessarily had in mind. Of the two of us, I was more the behind-the-scenes one, the executive assistant to Sukie's CEO. It was hard to imagine myself standing before a frenzied crowd, leading everyone in cheers.

Sukie was having none of it, however. "Come *on*, Lucy," she wheedled, drawing herself up to a sitting position. "When we talked about the Self-Improvement Program, we said we'd try to step outside our comfort zones, right? Try new things? Push the *envelope?*"

"I guess." Still lying on my stomach, I felt defenseless to argue with her. "All right ... let's try out then."

And so it was decided. The next morning I signed my name beneath Sukie's on the WHS Cheer Team Tryouts list, and we began practicing. Within a few weeks, we became well-acquainted with terms like *pike* and *herkie punch*, and I often woke up in the morning to painful complaints from muscles that had never before been asked to perform in such extreme ways.

Most of our practice sessions took place at the Hollisters'; we'd discovered that the living room was ideal for working on our form, since one entire wall was covered with mirrors. By mid-May, however, two weeks before tryouts, Sukie's mom had grown tired of all the jumping around. "Girls, I swear you're going to shake the light fixture right out of the ceiling," she admonished, looking upwards worriedly to where the shiny brass fixture was, indeed, swaying gently. "I hate to rain on your parade, but you're going to have to find somewhere else to practice."

"But Mo-*om*," Sukie protested, twisting her dark brown ponytail around one finger the way she always does when she's frustrated, "tryouts are a week from Wednesday; how are we supposed to work on our jumps if we can't watch ourselves?"

"You can watch each other," Mrs. Hollister told her firmly. "The living room is not a place for all this wild leaping around. How about the basement, or maybe the back yard?"

"Oh, fine," sighed Sukie, picking up her homemade practice pom-poms with a swish of annoyance. "But just so you know, the basement ceiling is too low. What if Lucy hits her head and her parents sue us?"

I nodded supportively, although I'd never known my parents to sue anyone.

Mrs. Hollister didn't look too concerned. "Hmm, well, try the back yard then," she advised.

Sukie sighed dramatically at this suggestion. "Have you ever tried jumping in grass?" she grumbled at her mother. "I guess we're stuck with the garage."

"Yep, sounds good," Mrs. Hollister agreed. If the image of us whacking our shins on stray bicycles and lawn mowers, or slipping in spilled motor oil worried her, she didn't show it. "Oh, and Sukie," she added, heading out of the room, "I just finished the Sanibel Island piece, if you wouldn't mind proofing it for me after Lucy leaves." Mrs. Hollister is a free-lance travel writer, and ever since we were in middle school she's been paying Sukie to edit her stuff. She says Sukie has a better eye than any professional editor she knows, and Sukie likes making the money, no matter how much she complains. Plus, I know it makes her feel good that her mother trusts her feedback on her writing.

Now, however, Sukie made her "save-me-*please*" face at me. I've always envied my best friend her light gray eyes; their color is almost ghostly, and everyone is always commenting on how unusual they are. My own eyes are boring blue—which my mom says is a perfect complement to my curly, reddish-brown hair and fair complexion. Even so, I wouldn't mind if there was something "unusual" about me, as long as it wasn't something strange like an extra toe or a streak of hair that grew in completely white. It's not like I want to stand out that much, but next to Sukie, I sometimes feel awfully *un*-remarkable.

"I think I'm ready for a break, anyway," I told Sukie now. The idea of continuing our practice in the humid space of the garage didn't sound especially appealing. "What've you got to drink?"

"Yeah, let's check it out," Sukie agreed. We headed towards the kitchen to see what it had to offer.

Despite all the time I've spent at Sukie's house over the years, the kitchen still comes as a surprise. The Hol-listers' house is always in a comfortable state of disarray (something my own mother would never tolerate), but the kitchen crosses over into the realm of disaster area. Sukie's mom uses one of the spare bedrooms as her official office, but her drafts and writing materials tend to spill out onto the kitchen table and countertops, where they join the general chaos of old mail, newspapers, unfolded laundry, and other miscellaneous items that end up piled on every available surface. Today, Sukie had to clear away a stack of reference books, a messily refolded map, a tower of clean bowls someone had unloaded from the dishwasher, and the family cat, Herman Muenster, from the kitchen table before we could find a place to sit and enjoy the bottled Starbucks Frappuccinos we found in the fridge.

"So, you think we'll make it?" Sukie asked, setting her bottle back down into the wet ring of condensation it had made on the oak kitchen table. I looked around, wondering where the Hollisters kept their coasters, or whether they even had any.

"What, the cheer team?" I asked rhetorically. Of course, I knew exactly what she meant. "I don't know … I'm not feeling too confident for myself, that's for sure." The question of whether or not we'd make one of the cheerleading squads was our favorite topic of conversation these days, and a debate we never tired of having. "Your jumps are a lot better than mine, so I'm sure *you'll* make it. Mine pretty much suck."

"Don't be ridiculous," Sukie scoffed. After two months, this script was sounding a bit worn, even to us. "I'm always forgetting the words, and besides, your arm motions are way tighter than mine. Your bones must be straighter or something. And as far as jumps go…your toe touch is amazing, and we both know it."

"Yeah, but your split jump is way better. And besides, you've got a voice like a foghorn."

"Well you've got the face of an angel…a *Hell's Angel*," Sukie retorted, and we both busted up laughing. That's one of the great things about Sukie; no one can think of a snappy comeback like she can.

"What are you two chickadees guffawing about now?" asked Mr. Hollister, coming into the kitchen. Sukie's dad is a pilot for Delta, so he's away for long stretches, then home in between. When he's around, he likes to putter in the kitchen or the yard; he's always showing us seedlings he's starting under a sunlamp in the basement, or cooking up some exotic new dish he ate on his last jaunt to Rome or Paris.

"Nothing, Dad," Sukie told him, still grinning. "Just goofing around."

"Uh-huh." Mr. Hollister seemed to be searching for something. He lifted the cover of the breadbox, then peered inside the fridge. "Do you know where your mother keeps the garlic?" he asked Sukie finally.

"Regular garlic or vampire garlic?" she asked. "If you're looking for vampire garlic, it's in the hall closet next to the wooden stakes."

Mr. Hollister smiled at Sukie fondly. "Silly girl," he said, winking at me, "everyone knows that vampire season is in the fall. Why, the werewolf kittens are barely stumbling out of their dens this time of year…"

"Werewolf *puppies*," Sukie corrected him. "And perhaps

you've forgotten that I'm the one who handled that awful unicorn infestation while you were gone?"

"Ah..." Mr. Hollister nodded. "That's *right*...I guess that explains why the lawn looks so unusually well-fertilized this spring."

I smiled patiently and took another sip of my Frappuccino. Sukie and her dad are always joking around like this; they're a regular Abbott and Costello. My dad and I get along fine, too, but it's not like I have a buddy-buddy relationship with him like Sukie and her dad have.

Now Mr. Hollister was rummaging around in one of the cupboards. "Aha!" he exclaimed, catching several spice jars as they came tumbling out. After returning them to the cupboard, he reached for something in the back and produced a small, square box containing a papery bulb of garlic. "There you are, my fragrant little friend!"

He turned to me and Sukie. "Actually," he told us, "I'm transplanting some rose bushes. Garlic is a great companion plant; keeps the bugs away."

Sukie raised her eyebrows. "Mom's not going to like it if the whole yard starts smelling like Mama Rosa's Italian Bistro."

"Look, Lady," Mr. Hollister told her in his gangster voice, "you just let me deal with the Feds." He closed the cupboard door, humming. "And how are you today, Lucy?"

"Um, I'm fine," I mumbled. Sukie's dad is tall and gray-haired. I'd never say this to Sukie, but he's actually pretty hot-looking for a dad. In fact, I always get a little tongue-tied when he talks to me directly. Even if Mr. Hollister weren't so good looking in that I-Fly-747s kind of way, it would still make me nervous when Sukie and her dad get to joking around with each other. Basically, I think I worry that they'll expect me to jump in and I won't be able to think of anything interesting to say.

"Sukie tells me that cheerleading tryouts are coming up soon," he said.

"Mm-hm," I nodded. *Note to self: Work on improving conversational skills.*

"Well, I'm sure you'll both do fine," Mr. Hollister predicted, tossing the garlic bulb into the air with one hand and snatching it back with the other. "You'll probably make the A-team or whatever it's called."

"It's called a *squad*, Dad," Sukie informed him. "*The A-Team* is that cheesy 1980s TV show." She drained the last of her drink and set the empty bottle down on the table. "Speaking of which," she said, turning to me, "we'd better head to the garage to finish practicing."

"Maybe we should call it a day," I suggested. The idea of jumping around with a belly full of sloshing Frappuccino didn't sound so great all of a sudden. "I probably ought to head home anyway; I'm supposed to work the dinner shift at the AO. And your mom wants you to read that article she wrote ..."

Sukie looked like she was going to protest, but changed her mind. "I guess we can pick it up tomorrow," she agreed. We walked outside to the driveway, where I'd left my bike. "I could give you a ride home in Olive," she offered, "except I don't know how we'd do with your bike."

I shrugged. "That's okay. I don't mind riding. Besides, how would I get to work without it?"

We'd both gotten our licenses in February, but since my mom was a stay-at-home mom, my parents weren't in the financial position to buy any of us kids a car. But even before I took my driver's test, I'd started saving up, and I was hoping to have enough for a decent used car by the time school started again in the fall. Along with the money Nana Lucy had sent for my birthday, I was counting on money from my hostess job at the Adobe Oven (aka the AO) to put me over the top.

The idea of driving myself to school next fall, battling for a parking place like most of the other kids my age, was truly sweet. My future car didn't have to be anything fancy; all I was hoping for was something with four wheels, a steering column, and most importantly, a motor. And something that allowed me to hook up my iPod, of course ... okay, maybe I did want a decent car.

Sukie's parents, on the other hand, had driven her straight to Stockman Motors car lot after she got her license. She'd picked out her new car, a pea-green Volkswagen Beetle she named Olive. Sukie often complained about being an only child, but it seemed to me that there were quite a few advantages.

As I pedaled up the driveway to my house on Chess Drive, a warm May breeze whispered that summer weather was just around the corner. It stirred feelings of both sadness and anticipation; the school year was ending, but the long, open days of summer lay ahead. Of course, I'd be putting in a lot of hours at the AO, but there'd still be plenty of time for bumming around with Sukie, working on our Self-Improvement Program, and—if everything worked out as expected—*cheerleading practice.*

Bikes, sporting gear, and lawn equipment littered our driveway, and inside the garage I could see my younger brother, Michael, moving dead leaves and other debris slowly across the garage floor with a heavy push broom. "Uh-oh," I said sympathetically. "What did you do?"

"Nothing." Michael shook his head, but looked miffed. "Dad said he'd pay me ten bucks if I 'helped' him clean out the garage. Then he conveniently got a long distance phone call and left me to do the whole thing myself."

"That sucks."

"Tell me about it."

I suppose I could have offered to help, but I was worn out from all the practicing at Sukie's. Parking my bike outside with the others, I went into the house.

My parents were sitting at the kitchen table, their usual coffee mugs sitting in front of each of them. "Hey, the garage looks good," I commented, thinking that maybe Dad had forgotten his promise to help Michael.

"Oh, Lucy, you're back." Mom smiled distractedly at me. "How was practice?" Dad only sat, staring at his coffee and looking upset.

"Uh, it was fine," I told Mom, suddenly uneasy. I couldn't remember the last time I'd seen my parents both looking so grim. "What's going on? Is something...wrong?"

two

Mom shook her head, but the little worried line between her eyes did nothing to reassure me. "Everything's fine, dear," she told me. "It's just that ... well, Daddy just got off the phone with Aunt Carol, and she's a little worried about Nana Lucy."

Nana Lucy is my dad's mother, who we only get to see a few times a year. While we live on the western edge of North Dakota, she lives hundreds of miles away in Minneapolis. She's my favorite grandmother—and the reason I'm named Lucy. Kellogg legend has it that when I was born, Dad took one look at my blue eyes and wavy hair already tinged with red and knew I would grow up to be the spitting image of Nana Lucy. He insisted that I be named after her, and nothing Mom said could change his mind. So, as a compromise, I was named Lucy Margaret Kellogg, since Margaret was the name of my mom's mother. I never got to meet Grandma Margaret; she passed away before I was born. Even Serena barely remembers her.

Nana Lucy is one of my favorite people in the world,

and I'm hers, of course. She lives in a little apartment in Minneapolis that looks out over Lake Calhoun. It's filled with all sorts of interesting things from her travels. After my grandfather, Sam Kellogg, passed away, Nana Lucy decided it was time that she see some things, and so she began signing up for "Senior Tours," the sort that take old people all over the United States, and even to other countries.

On one of her trips, she visited Europe with a group from her alma mater, Carleton College, and sent me a delicate snow globe from Paris that had a tiny replica of the Eiffel Tower inside. I keep it on my nightstand, and every time I look at it I picture a tiny Nana Lucy waving to me from the observation deck, a glass of elegant French champagne in her other hand.

Since I'm her namesake, Nana Lucy is always available by phone if I need advice, and she always sends me a special "From Lucy to Lucy" gift at Christmas. For years, it was beautiful porcelain dolls in elegant hand-stitched dresses. Even though they're not really my thing anymore, they still stand in a silent row across the top of my bookcase, posed like contestants in a beauty pageant.

Last year, thankfully, Nana Lucy finally broke with tradition and sent me two special presents: a necklace made of delicate milky pearls, and a tiny porcelain box in the shape of a cherry.

"No fair, you got two gifts," my little sister, Rachel, protested. She didn't look too upset, however. She'd just torn open her gift from Nana Lucy, which was a magic set, something she'd been wanting for months. I suspected, in fact, that Mom might have suggested the gift to Nana Lucy.

"You'll have to take special care of these, Lucy," Mom warned me as she examined to pearls. "I think this is the necklace that Grandpa Sam gave her for their fortieth wedding anniversary. It's an awfully expensive gift to give a teenage girl," she added, a faint note of disapproval in her voice.

"I *know*," I told her, slightly annoyed. Honestly. It's not like I'm six or anything. I've always taken good care of my "Lucy to Lucy" gifts. I was already planning to put the fragile porcelain box high up on a shelf in my room, and keep the pearls in Dad's fireproof office safe. Teenage girls don't wear a lot of pearls these days, but I felt good that Nana Lucy trusted me enough to give me some of her nice jewelry. It always seemed as if Mom felt a little funny about my special relationship with Nana Lucy, but maybe I was only imagining it. But now, in the kitchen, my mother's face was serious for a different reason.

"What do you mean, 'Aunt Carol is worried about Nana Lucy'?" I asked. "Why would she be worried?"

It had been a while since Nana had come to visit or sent any of her famous postcards, but I could easily bring to mind the luxurious scent of her Dior perfume and the scratchy feeling of her wool jacket against my cheek as she hugged me hello. When my grandfather was alive, they'd owned an upscale ladies' clothing store; even after they'd sold it and retired, Nana had continued to dress stylishly. She was a small woman, and sometimes she reminded me of one of the immaculately dressed dolls that stood atop my bookcase.

Mom opened her mouth to respond, but before she could, Dad pushed back his chair and got to his feet. "I'd better get outside," he muttered. "I promised I'd help Michael with the garage."

As the door closed behind Dad, our dog, Scooby, wandered sleepily out from under the table. Stretching one leg behind him, he opened his mouth and yawned a yawn so big it ended in a little yelp.

"Did we wake you, Scooby-Woobie?" Mom cooed, reaching down to lift him into her lap. Dad calls Scooby a "purebred brown dog," because he's the kind of dog that's such a mixture of breeds it's impossible to tell where he started out. Scooby has big dark eyes like a Chihuahua, but his coat is a disorganized mixture of brown and white fur that's of all different lengths growing in various directions, like whoever made Scooby kept losing their place.

Now Scooby settled against Mom with a satisfied sigh, and resumed his nap. "What's wrong with Nana?" I asked again, frustrated that no one was telling me anything.

Mom stroked Scooby and motioned for me to sit down in Dad's chair. "Well," she said when I was settled, "Aunt Carol called because she visited Nana Lucy last week, and found that she hadn't been keeping her place up like she usually does. You know how Nana's always been so particular about those things."

I nodded. Whenever we'd visited Nana Lucy's apartment in Triumph Towers, there was never a speck of dust or an unwashed dish anywhere in sight. When it came to standards for housekeeping, she was more strict than Mom.

"It wasn't just that things weren't tidy," Mom contin-ued. "Carol found spoiled food in the refrigerator, and when she went to make up the guest bed, she discovered that the entire linen closet was crammed with boxes of cereal and cookies."

I laughed in spite of myself. "Maybe Lunds had a sale." Nana always said that Lunds grocery store was the only place she'd ever buy her food. Still, it did seem a little strange that she'd buy so much cereal. As long as I'd known her, Nana Lucy had enjoyed tea and toast every day for breakfast. And the cookies... well, that was strange too.

Suddenly I felt agitated, like I was going to jump out of my skin. I wondered whether the Starbucks I'd had at Sukie's was having some kind of delayed effect.

Mom shook her head, still looking serious. "I'm afraid there's more, Lucy. Carol said that Nana's suitcases were still packed with dirty clothes from her last trip, and that the clothes she was wearing didn't seem very... fresh. She helped her get everything in order again, and cleaned up, but she felt funny leaving Nana by herself. And the worst thing," Mom added, as if everything else hadn't been enough, "was that when Carol got back to Madi-son and called Nana to tell her she'd arrived safely, Nana started talking about their visit to the Minneapolis Insti-tute of Arts. Nana said that she'd gone with 'a lovely young friend'; she didn't seem to remember that it had been Carol herself. Carol's wondering whether Nana Lucy even remembers much of her visit."

I was silent. There was no way to explain away all of that. "What does Dad think?" I asked.

"He's very worried, of course. It was hard for him to even talk about it. His grandmother, Nana's mother, had Alzheimer's disease."

"Alzheimer's disease?" I repeated. Nana Lucy couldn't have Alzheimer's disease; everyone was clearly overreacting. "But…isn't that where people leave the stove on and forget how to dress themselves? So what if Nana let the housekeeping slide and forgot to check the expiration date on the milk? Everyone *knows* she always eats out, anyway. And you know her sense of humor. I'm sure she was only teasing Aunt Carol."

It was hard for me to believe that Nana Lucy could suddenly have something like Alzheimer's disease. Not the Nana Lucy whose shoes always matched her bag and who always had funny, gossipy stories about the ladies in her Bunco club. "Besides," I said firmly, "aren't there doctors for these things? Can't they do some sort of test?"

Mom nodded. "Yes," she said, "You're right on both counts. That's part of the reason Carol called. She wants your father to talk to Nana Lucy about having an evaluation."

I thought for a minute. The image I had of a person with Alzheimer's disease was a far cry from my lively, fun grandmother with the sparkling blue eyes full of *joie de vivre* (something we'd learned about in French class).

"When is Dad going to talk to her?"

"He's trying to decide," Mom told me. "It won't be an easy conversation." She sighed. "There's another part. Whatever the outcome of the evaluation, Carol doesn't think Nana Lucy should be living alone anymore, especially since she's so far away from everyone. Carol and

Uncle Paul want her to come and live with them, but Paul's scheduled for back surgery in June and Carol doesn't think it's a great idea to have Nana Lucy moving in at the same time."

"So . . . what, then?" I asked. I couldn't imagine what Nana Lucy was going to say about everyone planning her life like this.

"Well, that's kind of a question right now," Mom said. "Your father and I are thinking that Nana Lucy could come to stay with us for a few months, just until Paul and Carol are ready for her. How bad could it be?" The last comment seemed directed more to herself than to me.

"Bad?" I repeated, surprised. "I think it's a *great* idea!" With Nana Lucy's fashion sense, she'd be an invaluable source of advice for the Self-Improvement Program. Besides, maybe after Nana Lucy spent some time with us she'd pull it together and whatever problems she was having would clear up. I smiled, thinking how nice it would be to have Nana Lucy in the house for the summer. "She can sleep with me," I volunteered.

Mom looked at me, but didn't say anything at first. Finally, she nodded. "We're taking things one step at a time," she murmured. "Once Nana gets here, we'll schedule her for the evaluation. Maybe there's some other explanation for all of this."

"There probably is," I agreed, trying to smile confidently, and wishing that my face could convince my heart that it was true.

BY AIR MAIL
PAR AVION
Royal Mail

Worldwide
postcard

Dolly Parton's Dixie Stampede Dinner & Show.

June 7th

Dearest Lucy,

Enjoying the musical offer-
ings here in Branson, Missouri.
This afternoon we attended a
performance by a nice young
man named Kenny Chestnut
(or something like that). He
pulled me from the crowd and
sang right to me... I think
I'll marry him if he asks me!
Remember this: I love you!
Nana Lucy
(the Future Mrs. Chestnut)

QUEBEC CIT
View from Lévis

GRAPHIC DESIGN ®

three

I'd agreed to work the dinner shift at the AO that night, so around 4:30 I tracked down my official AO uniform (a white peasant blouse that was too puffy for my taste, and a red cotton skirt with cheesy flowers embroidered around the hem) and hopped on my bike. Riding a bicycle across town in that sort of get-up generally invites pseudo-hilarious comments from people lucky enough to have cars, so I usually travel the back streets most of the way.

When I pulled up outside the Adobe Oven, I was greeted by the familiar strains of the mariachi CD that pretty much plays nonstop. Cherilyn and Donna, my two favorite waitresses, call it the *banda de sonido de mi vida*, the soundtrack of their lives. Even though I don't speak Spanish, in the two months since I'd started working at the AO I'd learned most of the songs through simple osmosis.

When I walked inside, both waitresses were standing by the hostess station, waiting for me. "Good news, *bonita*," Cherilyn said, her plump face gleaming. Of all the waitresses, Cherilyn is the only one who actually speaks Spanish.

"Frank found religion and decided to give me a raise?" I suggested hopefully. Frank was the manager, and while I knew a raise was unlikely, there was nothing wrong with optimism.

Donna rolled her eyes. "If anyone should be getting a raise, it's me," she snorted. "When I got home last night my feet were so tired I could barely push the vacuum." Donna and Cherilyn were always complaining about their feet, and I was sorry I'd unintentionally introduced the topic.

"Don't even get me started, Dee," Cherilyn commiserated. She opened her mouth to top Donna's sore foot story, so I interrupted.

"Well, what's up?"

It worked; Cherilyn seemed to remember where she'd started. She nudged Donna. "Do you want to tell her or should I?"

Donna forgot about her feet and grinned, the friendly creases around her eyes deepening. "Frank hired a new dishwasher," she told me. "Looks like he's about your age and *awfully* cute … we thought maybe you should go back to the kitchen and say hello."

Ever since I'd started at the AO, Donna and Cherilyn were always badgering me about my not having a boyfriend. It appeared that they'd finally hit upon a prospect right under our own fake-clay roof. I don't know why either one of them was on such a mission to find me a boyfriend; to hear them tell it, neither of them has had great histories with men. Donna has a cap on the broken front tooth her ex-husband gave her and says she'll never get married again, while Cherilyn has three kids from two different fathers; both fathers are currently serving time in the penitentiary. Apparently she hasn't learned, however. Even though it's supposed to be a big secret, everyone at the AO knows that she and Frank are hooking up. Donna and I always give each other a look when they disappear to the downstairs office for a "meeting."

As I opened my mouth to ask a few questions about the hotness quotient of the new dishwasher, the front door jangled a warning. The dinner rush was about to begin, and the waitresses scattered. Frank doesn't like them hanging around the cash register; he says it looks unprofessional. Frank's a couple years younger than Cherilyn and a lot younger than Donna, which makes it seem strange that he's in charge. Everyone goes along with it, even though some of his rules seem silly, even to me.

"Welcome to the Adobe Oven." I smiled sweetly, greeting the two couples who had come in. "Will it be four today?" They seemed impressed with my counting abilities, and nodded as I pulled four menus from the menu rack. "Did you have a seating preference?"

I seated them at a table in Donna's section, then walked back across the restaurant, trying not to be obvious about glancing through the serving window into the kitchen. Unfortunately, Lupe, the head cook, and Julio, his assistant, were blocking my view of the new dishwasher.

"Hey there, beautiful," Doug the bartender called from behind the bar, where he was busy refilling the condiment bins. "What's new?"

I smiled at him. For an older guy, Doug was pretty cute,

and always fun to flirt with. "Not much," I called. "What's up with you?"

"Still taking on oxygen," he replied with a wink. "Catch." He tossed me a green olive, which I caught in mid-air.

I popped it in my mouth. "*Gracias, amigo.*" He grinned. I like Doug a lot; when the restaurant is slow, he'll sometimes surprise me with a colorful, fruity cocktail decorated with umbrellas. Alcohol-free, of course. He knows I'm only sixteen.

"Anytime, *mamacita.*"

When I arrived back at the hostess station, I tried to figure out how to take another shot at checking out the new dishwasher. There was no harm in looking, after all, especially since both Donna and Cherilyn seemed in agreement that he was worth seeing.

Aside from any self-serving reasons, I was glad for Lupe that Frank had finally hired someone to help out. The old dishwasher was a slacker named Charles, who had been fired after Lupe caught him swishing his arm around in the salsa barrel clear up to his hairy armpit. Under Lupe's interrogation, Charles finally admitted that he'd been fishing for his lighter, which he'd accidentally dropped into the salsa. Frank had fired him on the spot and told Julio to pour the whole barrel of salsa down the disposal. Lupe was pretty ticked about it, since he'd just finished making the new batch of salsa that morning.

Charles' departure meant that Julio was drafted into the role of dishwasher, leaving Lupe with no assistant to help him with food prep when things got busy, as they often did. Donna told me that Lupe had threatened to quit unless Frank found him a new dishwasher.

The front door swung open again and stayed open as the trickle of customers became the steady stream of a typical Saturday night dinner rush. I was so busy seating customers and ringing up tickets that for the next two hours I didn't have any time to think about what was going on back in the kitchen, other than to ask, "And how was everything?" when customers came up to pay their bills.

"Great!" or "Man, I'm stuffed!" were the usual responses. Being the hostess at a restaurant where the food was fantastic wasn't too difficult. Although the AO was the only Mexican restaurant in Williston, it would have killed the competition had there been any. Lupe's homemade tortillas were soft and fragrant, and he personally chose only the freshest produce from the local vendors. His *moles* were redolent with spices and people came from miles around to order his *cocina especial*.

I knew I was Lupe's favorite; he often called me back to the kitchen to sample a new batch of salsa, and had even given me the recipe for it when I'd asked. "What?" Donna exclaimed indignantly when I told her. "He never gives anyone that recipe!" She looked so disgruntled that I didn't dare tell her that lemon juice was the secret ingredient in Lupe's *mariscos* tacos.

The flow of customers hit a momentary lull around eight thirty, leaving me with a few minutes to lean on the counter, catch my breath, and think about things that were lurking around the edges of my mind, muttering impatiently for attention.

I was still digesting the news about Nana Lucy. I'd also been thinking, on the ride to work, that Sukie and I didn't have much more time to practice for cheerleading tryouts. As much as we'd talked the subject to death, we had no idea how many girls were trying out this year. What we *did* know was that Sarah Kenwood and her friends were trying out. Everything about those girls was perfect; perfect clothes, perfect hair, perfect bodies... no Self-Improvement Program needed. There were four girls in Sarah's group: Lauren, Fiona, Peyton, and Sarah herself. If they were all trying out, it pretty much guaranteed that they'd be chosen for four of the eight available spots on the cheer team next fall. "That sucks," I muttered, thinking out loud.

"What's that, honey?" Donna asked. She'd appeared out of nowhere. Tucking her order pad into the pocket of her skirt, she leaned on the hostess desk, looking worn out. In the light from the lamp hanging overhead, I could see the fine film of perspiration that glistened on her forehead and dampened her blonde hair at the temples. "Whew, I'm getting too old for this," she sighed, as she always did.

"Oh, Donna, you're not old," I assured her, as I always did when she said this. Sometimes it seemed like life was just a series of scripts. The truth was, everyone at the AO seemed kind of old to me; it wasn't like a normal food service job at the Burger Barn or Dairy Queen, where most of the workers were kids and the only adults were management. On the other hand, I liked everyone I worked with at the AO, and being the hostess made me feel more mature.

"So, did you get a look at the new guy yet?" she asked, "He's a cutie and a half."

I shook my head. "It's been so crazy in here that I forgot all about Mr. Right with the dishpan hands."

"Nothing wrong with a man with dishpan hands," Donna pointed out. "Far better than beer elbow." She mimed bringing a bottle to her lips.

I nodded, figuring she should know. "All right," I told her, "you've convinced me. If you watch for customers, I'll go back to the kitchen and check out the new suds muffin."

"Suds muffin?" Donna cracked up. "I can't wait to tell Cherilyn that one! You're funny, girl!"

I left her, still chuckling, at the hostess station and made my way towards the kitchen. Through the food service opening, I could see Lupe scraping away at the grill while Julio worked the set-up area. There was usually a final evening rush around ten, but now they had some down time to get everything reorganized.

Behind Lupe, I could see the new dishwasher toiling away at the sink, rinsing dishes. Even from a distance, I could see muscular shoulders under his gray T-shirt, the back of which was stained with a damp V of perspiration. His hair was dark, too, and curled damply against his neck in the back.

"Hey there, Chef," I greeted Lupe as I came through the door into the kitchen. "So you lived to fight another day?"

A grin lit up Lupe's heat-flushed face; the kitchen was hot as a steam bath. "Eh, eh, it's the hostess with the mostest!" he called out fondly, as he always did when I dropped by the kitchen for a visit. "Are you hungry, *Lucita?* How about a nice *quesadilla . . .*"

"Thanks, Lupe, but I just dropped by to say hello," I told him. "I hear Frank finally found you a new dishwasher."

Lupe scowled. "He is too young," he told me gruffly, as if the dishwasher wasn't standing right behind him, within earshot of every word.

Before I could find out what Lupe considered to be the minimum qualifying age to scrub pots and pans, the new dishwasher finished with rinsing out the sink and turned, stripping off his heavy rubber gloves. "Can I take a break?" he asked Lupe. "I really need to use the john."

Lupe threw his hands up in the air hopelessly, as if this confirmed every doubt he'd had about the new dishwasher. "Go, go," he ordered hopelessly.

The dishwasher started to leave, but stopped when he saw me. "Hey," he said. "I know you...you're *Lucy*, right?"

I stared at him, my mouth open, but no available breath to assist in a response. "Uh, yeah," I managed, finally. "Well, um, I'd better go back to..." I was momentarily unable to think what to call my post at the front of the restaurant. Spinning on my heel, I turned and fled. I nearly knocked over Julio, who was on his way to the big fridge.

Donna was gone when I arrived back at the hostess station. I saw her across the room, seating an elderly couple that had come in for a late dinner. It was just as well; I needed some time to regroup. The dishwasher had been right—he looked familiar to me, too. In fact, I knew *exactly* who he was: Sukie's arch enemy, aka He Who Shall Not Be Named.

four

Our history with He Who Shall Not Be Named dated back to our freshman year. Sukie had developed a huge crush on him the first day of school, when he'd turned up in our freshman algebra class. "Ohmigod," she breathed. "Lucy, I think I've just met the father of my children."

I followed her gaze until I saw where she was looking. "Well, you haven't exactly *met* him yet," I pointed out.

Sukie dismissed me with a flap of her hand. "Nothing more than a detail, Sister," she scoffed. I'd seen that look on her face before; it was the look she got when she practiced her flute in the weeks before blowing everyone else out of the water in the middle school band competition. Seeing that look, I was pretty sure that He Who Shall Not Be Named didn't have a chance.

From that moment on, Sukie waged a whole-hearted campaign to get HWSNBN's attention. She greeted him every morning with a carefree and flirtatious "Hey, there," made dry, sarcastic comments in class until the teacher was fed up with her, and called me nightly to discuss strategy.

When two weeks had passed and HWSNBN didn't seem to be showing Sukie any more attention than anyone else, she pulled out all the stops. After class one day, she casually caught up with him while everyone was on their way out the door, and tugged on his arm. Out in the hallway a minute later, I watched in admiration as Sukie chatted with him like she did it every day of the week.

I wasn't the only one watching, either; I noticed that Sarah Kenwood had slowed her pace to keep an eye on what was happening. When she was almost to the end of the hall, she stopped and bent down to retie the laces on her Skechers, but behind the curtain of perfect blonde hair I could see that her violet-blue eyes were trained on the conversation .

Suddenly, Sukie was coming towards me, a triumphant smile on her flushed face. "His cell number!" she mouthed, pointing to where she'd written it in her notebook, and I felt a nervous flutter in my chest. I suspected that Sarah Kenwood had some designs of her own on HWSNBN, and I hoped that Sukie knew what she was up against.

"How'd you get his number so quick like that?" I knew Sukie had nerve, but even so, I was impressed.

She laughed. "I said I was confused about the material for the test next week, and asked him if I could call him to ask him about some of the problems."

"What'd he say?"

"He said, 'Uh, oh ... well ... I guess so,'" Sukie repeated. Her imitation didn't make him sound very enthusiastic about the idea.

"Wow," I said anyway. "So, you're going to call him then?"

She considered. "I think I'll text him a couple times first," she said. "It doesn't seem as pushy as calling. You know guys... they like to feel that they're in control."

I walked along silently. The truth was, I had zero experience in this realm, but neither did Sukie. She was putting on a good act, though.

"Besides," Sukie added, "texting is a little sexier than calling, don't you think?"

I nodded in agreement, even though I couldn't actually argue that point either. Since a cell phone was something my parents deemed unnecessary for a freshman in high school, cell phone etiquette wasn't a concern of mine. Sukie, of course, had been carrying a state-of-the-art cell phone ever since we were in seventh grade.

As we continued down the hall, with Sukie jabbering away, I caught a glimpse of Sarah Kenwood falling into pace beside HWSNBN, and together they rounded the corner.

Later that night, Sukie called me (on my house phone, of course). "So, I just sent him a text," she told me proudly. "And he sent one back."

"Really? What did you say?"

"Well, I told him I was still having trouble with my math problems, since that was supposedly the reason I needed his number."

"Good point," I agreed.

"So then he offered to explain them to me, and I said how about tomorrow during our sixth period study hall."

"Oh my god, Sukie! You've got nerve."

"Yeah." I could hear Sukie's smile over the phone lines. "We're going to ask for a pass to the library."

This was unprecedented success; I couldn't believe that Sukie had gone straight from texting to an actual almost-date. "Wow," I told her. "That's incredible."

"No kidding. I suppose I'm going to have to think of some questions about the material now."

"Uh-huh." Sukie has the best math brain of anyone I know, so it was kind of hilarious to imagine her pretending that she didn't.

I was still nervous, though, at lunch the next day. I'd noticed Sarah Kenwood staring at us from the popular table in the lunch room, and the look on her face wasn't friendly.

"Sukie," I muttered, "Sarah Kenwood is giving you the snake eye. I think she might have a thing for him, too."

Sukie glanced over at Sarah's table, but Sarah had turned away and was laughing with Lauren Simmons as if she couldn't care less what we inferior beings were up to. "Hey, as far as I'm concerned, it's every woman for herself," she said. "May the hottest chick win."

There was no use pointing out to Sukie that Sarah Kenwood didn't have to compete with Sukie or anyone else. She was in a class by herself—the kind of girl who was so pretty she seemed like a separate kind of being altogether. Sukie knew this as well as I did, and I supposed she just didn't want to believe that Sarah might be after him, too. It would have been too much to think she was up against a goddess like Sarah Kenwood. Who wants to compete with *that?*

Later that afternoon, I ran into Sukie again. She'd spent sixth period being "tutored" by HWSNBN and was literally glowing. "I can't even describe it," she whispered, still a little breathless. "He's even hotter than he looks in class. His hair, his eyes..." She trailed off, overcome at the memory.

"What did you guys talk about?"

She looked exasperated. "Algebra, of course," she reminded me. "I'm sure he was impressed by how quickly I picked it up."

"Oh, yeah. But did you talk about anything personal?"

"Not really," she admitted. "It was mostly math. Oh wait, he did say that he's going bowling tomorrow. I asked him if he wanted to get together again to study some more and he said he already had plans. So I said maybe Sunday, since we have that test on Monday."

"Oh, well, that's good, I guess. At least your relationship has a future."

Sukie looked momentarily doubtful. "Well, he didn't say 'yes' for sure, but he seemed open to the idea." She thought for a moment, then seemed to make a decision. "I think I'll text him tomorrow to set it up. Once we study for a little while, maybe I'll suggest we could grab dinner or something sometime. Then hopefully he'll ask me out."

I nodded, feeling a little glimmer of envy. We were only a few weeks into our freshman year and already Sukie was halfway to having a boyfriend. It didn't seem fair that things always worked out for Sukie. Still, she'd been my best friend since the third grade, and I was happy for her. Maybe she and HWSNBN could even find *me* a boyfriend. I'd noticed he hung around with Tyler Driscoll, for example, who was fairly hot himself, in my opinion. I let my mind drift ahead to picture the four of us going on dates together, riding the go-carts at the Missouri Valley Speedway, playing miniature golf, going to the movies, sharing a double order of chili fries at the Burger Barn.

"Now we'll have to find *you* a man," Sukie said, reading my thoughts.

That night, Sukie slept over at my house and our conversation was dominated by talk of Sukie's future with HWSNBN. The next morning, Serena gave us a ride to the mall where we shopped for a new top that Sukie could wear during her upcoming study date with him. When we arrived back home, we sprawled on the floor of the bedroom I shared with Rachel (this was before Serena left for college) and talked idly about life in general. I brought up the subject of Tyler Driscoll, and Sukie immediately suggested that setting me up with him should be Phase Two in Operation HWSNBN.

Around two o'clock, Sukie dug in her purse for her cell phone, which she'd decorated with glimmering orange rhinestones. "He's probably at the bowling alley right now," she announced, flopping back onto her stomach next to me. "I think I'll text him and see what time he wants to get together tomorrow. To study," she added, giving me a wink.

I watched as she worked the keypad of her phone,

punching in the message. She tilted the screen so I could read it.

HEY THERE! HWZ YR BWLING AVG?
STIL WN2 STDY 2MRW?

"Sounds good," I agreed, getting to my feet. "Do you want something to drink?" I was suddenly thirsty, and a tall glass of soda sounded fabulous.

"Sure," she nodded, her head bent over her phone's keypad as she pushed buttons rapidly. "Okay... I'm sending it."

"All right. I'll be back in a minute." I headed out of the room. In the kitchen, I took my time, filling two glasses with ice and splitting a can of root beer between them.

When I returned to the bedroom, I found Sukie sitting up, her back against the bed. Her thumbs were working the keypad again. "Did he text back?" I asked.

Sukie nodded, but didn't take her eyes off of what she was doing. I set a glass of root beer on the bedside table near her and picked up my iPod. I'd put the ear buds in my ears, and was just scrolling through my options, when I glanced up and saw that Sukie's face was red as a beet.

"What's wrong?" I asked, pulling the ear buds out. "Sukie?"

My friend looked up at me, her gray eyes filled with a mixture of anger and hurt, both emotions swimming behind tears.

"What the...?" I grabbed the phone from her and looked at the screen.

RB@U, BTCH

I looked at Sukie, confused, and she reached out to take the phone back from me. She pushed a few buttons, then handed it back, showing me where I could find *Messages Sent* and *Messages Received*.

Sukie: HEY THERE! HWZ YR BWLING AVG? STIL WN2 STDY 2MRW?

HWSNBN: WHZ THIS?

Sukie: SKIE HLLSTR, U MRN

HWSNBN: O

Sukie: HI

Sukie: 2MRW?

HWSNBN: LSTN, SRY F I GVE U TH RONG IDEA, BT I HAVE A GF.

HWSNBN: UR NT MY TYP ANYWY. I USLY LKE GRLS THT R MR GOODLKNG.

Sukie: DNT FLATTER YRSLF; IM NT NTRSTD IN U

Sukie: N FCT, >U

HWSNBN: RB@U, BTCH

"Oh, Sukie." I handed the phone back to her. "I'm so sorry."

I didn't totally understand all of what I'd read, but I got the gist of the conversation. Not only did HWSNBN not want to study with my best friend the next day, but apparently he was a rude, hurtful bastard. And actually, although I didn't know what ">U" meant, I was pretty sure Sukie had also said something pretty rude, text-wise.

"What does 'RB@U' mean?" I asked. I didn't have to ask about "BTCH."

"Right back at you," Sukie spat, wiping tears from her eyes with the heels of both hands. "What a disappointing cliché *he* turned out to be, huh? 'Not his type'... jerk." She closed the phone with a sharp snap and tossed it into the purse. "I guess that's the end of that." She said it dismissively, but as her best friend, I could hear the ragged edge of hurt in her voice. Then she added dramatically, "That's the end of *him*. To us, he's the equivalent of... Voldemort."

Sukie had read all the Harry Potter books, several times. Once she'd discovered them, she'd been one of those kids who stood in line to get the latest edition the moment it came out. "Like with Voldemort, we shall never speak his name again," she decreed, taking a deep breath and straightening her back. She held out her pinkie to me, how we'd made promises to each other since the third grade.

I was her friend, and it was my job to stand behind her. "All right, then," I told her, linking my pinkie through hers. "We'll never speak his name again."

And that is how he became *persona-no-longer-hotta,* aka, He Who Shall Not Be Named.

BY AIR MAIL
PAR AVION
Royal Mail

Worldwide
postcard

Family
14403-
Oak Park

The Golden Gate Hotel and Casino,
the oldest hotel and casino in Las Vegas

September 19th

Lucy Darling,
We've only been in Las Vegas for one day and already I've seen the most magical performance of Cirque du Soleil and won $40 in the nickel slot machines! No time to write more; Lady Luck is saving me a seat at the blackjack tables... cross your fingers and knock on wood!
Remember this: I love you!
Nana L.

QUEBEC CIT
View from Lévis

Lucy,
For sea
card of the
because I
wonderful
apartment
even though
traveler is
Dorothy a
Oz, there
like from
End ad
I hear y

GRAPHIC DESIGN ®

five

Pedaling home from work, I admired the sunset and debated whether I should call Sukie and tell her that I'd be spending my summer working with He Who Shall Not Be Named. I was so absorbed in my thoughts that I barely noticed when a carload of boys drove by, hooting at me in my ultra-sexy AO outfit.

By the time I pulled my bike into the driveway, though, I'd made the decision to wait on telling Sukie about the "situation" at work. There was no reason to upset her with cheerleading tryouts coming up, and I suspected that the very mention of his name would probably reignite her fury. She might even expect me to quit working at the AO, which would pretty much ruin any chance of getting a car by fall. I promised myself I'd tell her as soon as tryouts were over—probably while we were crying into ice cream sundaes and consoling each other over our mutually humiliating failure to make any of the cheerleading squads.

When I came in the back door to the kitchen, Rachel

was sitting on the kitchen counter eating a banana Popsicle. "Hey," I greeted her.

"Hi...how was work?"

"Oh, it was *oodles* of fun," I replied dryly. Since Rachel is only eleven and I'm her older sister, she still thinks I'm the coolest person in the world, poor thing. I remember when I felt the same way about Serena, even though she pretended I was a huge pain in her neck.

"Listen," Rachel said. "I've been thinking...I've decided I'm going to work at the OA too. When I'm old enough to get a job."

"That's AO," I corrected her. "Not OA."

Her face grew red. "Uh, yeah...the *AO*...that's what I meant. Anyway, I'm going to be a hostess just like you. I'll bet it's awesome."

"Maybe you should be a waitress instead," I advised. "Waitresses make tips." I didn't bother explaining that she couldn't be a waitress at the Adobe Oven; since they served alcohol, waitresses had to be twenty-one. She'd have to settle for working at the Country Buffet or Trapper's Kettle, where waitresses only had to be fifteen.

"Oh, okay...that's what I'll do." Rachel was looking at me like I was her personal Buddha. I pictured her writing in her diary that night: *Today Lucy, the Great Wise One, prophesied that I will someday become a waitress.*

"Or maybe you'll do something entirely different when you get into high school," I added, feeling uneasy that I might be unintentionally determining the career course of my sister's life. "Like, maybe you'll start out as a lifeguard at Harmon Park Pool, or work in one of the jewelry stores, or ..."

I stopped, seeing Rachel's eyes grow wide at the scope and breadth of my expectations for her. "You know what, Rach?" I said, "That's all still four years away. Don't even worry about it right now. I'll even help you decide where to apply when the time comes, if you want me to."

She looked relieved. "Really? You will?"

"Yep. Hey, do you know where Mom is? Or Dad?" I wanted to see if there were any updates on the Nana Lucy situation.

Rachel shrugged, then jumped down off the counter and threw the stick from her Popsicle in the trash under the sink. "They went for a drive. Mom said they had to talk about some things. Michael's supposed to be watching me until you get home."

"Well, then, where's he at?"

"Where else? On the computer."

Rachel was right. I found Michael in my dad's office in front of the computer. He was IMing with his girlfriend, Hanna, while they made faces at each other via webcam; when I came into the room, he looked up and showed me that he'd drawn a mustache and goatee on his face with a black marker. Looking over his shoulder, I could see Hanna laughing her head off.

"Hey," he said, turning back to the screen.

"Hey," I responded, sinking into the corner armchair. "Did Mom and Dad tell you about Nana Lucy?"

"You mean that she might be coming to stay with us for a while?" Michael muttered, typing while he was talking. "I hope you know they're planning on her crashing in your room."

I nodded. "That's fine with me. Did they tell you that Aunt Carol thinks she might have Alzheimer's disease?"

"Uh ... yeah." *Clickety-clickety-clickety* went the keyboard beneath his flying fingers.

"I don't believe it though. Nana Lucy's too ... *with it* to have Alzheimer's."

"Uh-huh." Michael was reading something Hanna had written, and now he snorted and started typing again.

I gave up trying to have a serious conversation with him and went up to my room. It had only become "my room" after Serena left for the University of Montana. Initially, my parents had talked about making her room into a guest room, since our guests generally had to sleep on the sofa or at the Westward Ho Motel. I'd shared a room with Rachel for years and was just beginning to think things would stay that way when, to my surprise, Serena began campaigning for me. "Lucy deserves it," she'd said. "Every teenage girl should have her own room." In the end, my parents had seen the light and allowed me to move in.

Mom even let me redecorate. I'd painted the walls a soft lavender color called "Daydream" and chosen a pale green satin duvet for the bed. After I'd added some throw pillows in shades of peach and purple, even Mom said I'd done a professional job of decorating. The whole effect was so fresh and pretty that it made me happy every time I opened the door.

Now I peeled off my skirt and peasant top and threw them on top of the hamper, making a mental note to carry the entire thing down to the laundry room later. It never took long for the smell of Mexican food to fill my entire room if I left my work clothes lying around. I changed into a T-shirt and a pair of boxers. I was ready to relax. It was Saturday night, but after a busy shift at work I didn't feel like doing anything besides chilling in front of the television.

An hour later, I was curled up on the sofa watching an MTV reality show when the telephone rang. And rang. And rang. "Somebody get that!" I hollered, too comfortable to consider moving. "RACHEL!" I yelled, "Answer the phone!" After two more rings I gave an exasperated snarl and struggled out of my cozy nest to scramble for the phone.

"Hello?" I barked.

There was a pause, then Nana Lucy's voice on the other end. "Oh, dear," she said uncertainly. "I'm trying to reach the Kellogg household ..."

"Nana Lucy?" I immediately felt bad. "Sorry I yelled. I just wasn't sure if I was going to make it to the phone before it stopped ringing."

"I hope I didn't interrupt anything important," she said.

"Of course not. I was just watching TV."

"Ah, yes," Nana Lucy chuckled. "The 'boob tube.' We used to call it that because we thought too much TV-watching made people stupid, but now it's because of all the indecent programs they show." It was the kind of observation Nana Lucy always made, and instantly I felt less worried about her.

"You're probably right about that," I agreed. "So, Nana Banana, what's new with you?"

Nana Lucy made a *tsk*-ing sound. "Well, not much

really. Although your Aunt Carol seems to think I'm losing my marbles."

I chewed my lip. It was probably better to have the subject right out in the open, but now that it was, I didn't really know what to say about it. "Well, what do you think, Nana?" I asked finally. "You're *not*, are you?"

Nana Lucy sighed. "I'm seventy-three years old, my dear. It's not natural to expect someone my age to have the brain of a twenty-year-old, is it?"

"I guess not." She had a point there. In sociology class, we'd learned about the aging process and how cognitive abilities changed over a person's life span.

"Even if I've become a bit forgetful, I don't honestly think that it's anything to get panicky about. I've got a trip coming up to North Carolina in August, and now Carol wants me to cancel it. It really rankles me, Lucy; I've already paid the deposit and everything. But she's convinced your father that I shouldn't be traveling alone. I won't be alone, I told her. I'd be with an entire busful of gray-haired people who can't remember things any better than I can. I'm not sure what she thinks is going to happen; maybe that I'm so addle-brained that I'd get off at some rest stop and wander away, or some other such nonsense."

"Huh," I said neutrally. Nana sounded all right to me, and I was starting to hope that maybe everyone was overreacting. Still…maybe *that* was normal for Alzheimer's disease. I made a mental note to do an Internet search after Michael got off the computer, just to see what I could find out. On the other hand, part of me felt like I didn't want to read things that might convince me that Aunt Carol was right.

"At any rate," Nana continued, "your father left a message inviting me to come out for a visit, and I'm calling to accept the invitation. I haven't been out that way for quite some time, and I've missed seeing you all. Especially my favorite namesake, Miss Lucy Kellogg!"

"I've missed you too, Nana," I told her, smiling. "It's awesome that you're coming to see us for a while."

"Awesome is right," Nana replied. "Now catch me up on what's new and exciting in your life these days!"

As I prattled on to Nana Lucy about the end of school, my job at the AO, and cheerleading tryouts, guilt was tugging at my conscience. I was relieved that she sounded so normal, of course, but I also had a sneaking suspicion that she only knew half of her children's plan for her. My grandmother thought her visit to North Dakota would only be that, a visit. She had no idea that Dad and Aunt Carol intended it to be the first stop on a journey away from her apartment in Minneapolis and away from the familiar life that she knew. I felt like a trick was being played on my unsuspecting grandmother, and if I didn't say anything, then I'd be a part of it.

And yet, I couldn't be the one to tell her the whole truth. I just *couldn't*. I would just have to hope that the evaluation would show that she didn't have Alzheimer's, and then everyone could admit they'd been crazy to worry. Nana Lucy could get back on a plane to Minneapolis and arrive home in time to pack her bags for North Carolina, none the wiser about what her family had plotted and planned behind her back.

At least, I hoped that was how it would turn out.

six

The third Monday in May dawned bright and sunny like any other late-spring day, except that for me and Sukie it was the most important day of our lives: WHS cheerleading tryouts, and hopefully the day that our Self-Improvement Program really took off. The following Friday marked the end of the school year, which meant that whoever made the cheer team would soon be free to spend the rest of the summer learning cheers and practicing their routines for next fall's sporting events. It was also the day when Nana Lucy was scheduled to arrive from Minneapolis, but I'd hardly had time to think about that yet.

"Nervous, sweetie?" Mom asked me at breakfast. She handed the milk carton to Rachel, who had already filled her cereal bowl with Lucky Charms.

I took a swallow of juice to dislodge the bite of peanut-butter toast that was stuck in my throat, and nodded. "We probably won't make it," I cautioned for the umpteenth time. "Really, there will be lots of people trying out."

"I'm not worried," Rachel said confidently. She was

using her spoon to pick the pink marshmallow hearts out of her cereal first, as she always does, and now she looked up at me proudly. "You'll probably be the best one there."

Mom smiled at me. "Whether you make it as a cheerleader or not, you'll always have your #1 Fan." She leaned over to drop a kiss on the top of Rachel's head.

"Don't think I don't appreciate it," I said.

A half hour later I arrived at school to find Sukie already waiting anxiously at my locker. "It took me forever to fall asleep last night," she told me, "and when I finally did, I dreamt that we were doing our routine for the judges, but when I opened my mouth, I couldn't remember the cheer! Not one word!"

I laughed. "That's not going to happen," I assured her. I wondered how it would be possible to make it through an entire day of classes, much less learn anything. "They ought to hold tryouts first thing in the morning," I muttered, "to put everyone out of their misery."

"No kidding," Sukie agreed. "Today is going to be a complete waste."

The day passed slowly, but finally it was three thirty and the last bell rang. "All cheerleading candidates please report to the main gymnasium," a voice broadcast ominously over the school's intercom.

"Ohmigod … ohmigod … ohmigod," Sukie was chanting when I got to her locker. Her hands were clammy when she grabbed mine and squeezed. "This is it."

"I know." I squeezed back, although I wasn't actually feeling as nervous as I'd expected to be. After all the weeks of planning and practicing for this moment, the idea that it had finally arrived wasn't sinking in.

We deposited our books in Sukie's locker and made our way down the teeming hallway towards the auditorium. Along the way, I could hear voices calling out to other girls. Shouts of "Good luck, Sophie!" or "I know you'll make it, Bree!" flew through the air over our heads, and it occurred to me that really the only people who were rooting for me and Sukie were each other. *It doesn't matter*, I told myself. Sukie was the only person I needed in my corner, and I knew it was the same for her.

At the auditorium, we changed into T-shirts and shorts in the girls' locker room and headed upstairs. When we entered the gym, I saw that there were at least thirty girls milling around or standing in small, nervous clusters at the foot of the bleachers. Other students were gathering in the bleachers to watch, and I could see the three judges standing across the gym by what I supposed was the judges' table.

One of the senior cheerleaders was handing out printed numbers that we were supposed to pin to our T-shirts so that the judges could identify us. "Here you go," she said, handing Sukie and me our numbers and two safety pins.

Suddenly, someone called my name. "Lucy! Lucy!" I looked up into the bleachers and saw Mom and Rachel waving. If they'd told me they were planning to come and watch tryouts, I'd have told them not to, but now I was glad to see them there. I waved back, then pretended to be gnawing my fingernails in terror to make them laugh.

The microphone blared feedback and everybody

jumped. "Girls, can you please line up along the bleachers?" one of the judges asked, when it had cleared. "We'd like to get started."

My number was twelve, which made me happy because twelve is one of my lucky numbers. Of course, twenty-three is my *real* lucky number, but that would have been too much to hope for. Since she was sitting beside me, Sukie got number thirteen. That alone might have made some people nervous, but fortunately it's not the sort of thing Sukie usually worries about. In fact, she was staring off into space and almost seemed to be in a trance. "Suke?" I said, and was relieved when she turned and smiled.

"I'm centering my chakra," she explained.

"Your *what*-ra?"

Before she could answer, the judges began to call out numbers. Suddenly I realized I *was* a little nervous after all. Before settling themselves behind their table, the judges had explained that they wanted to see each girl's jumps individually at first, and then they would begin the group cheers. We'd all learned the same cheer in phys ed class, and this would allow the judges to mix and match groups until they came up with a squad of girls who worked well together.

First up was Megan Fisher, a tiny blonde girl who I didn't know well. "I'd hate to go first," I whispered to Sukie, who nodded in grave agreement. The entire gym watched as Megan spoke briefly with the judges, then proceeded to show them her jumps: *Split jump ... herkie ... pike ... toe touch ... side hurdler*. Megan's silky ponytail leapt and bounced behind her as she completed the series.

"That was pretty good," I whispered, as we watched Megan come running back to her spot on the bench.

"Naw...your jumps are lots better than hers," my loyal friend whispered back.

There were cheers each time the first few girls finished jumping, but by contestant number seven, the crowd had grown bored and was beginning to murmur amongst themselves. I glanced up at Mom and Rachel, and Rachel flashed me a grin and the thumbs-up sign. "This is going to go on forever," Sukie muttered, and I nodded in agreement.

Before I knew it, however, the judges were calling for contestant number twelve, and Sukie gave me a nudge with her elbow. "Good luck!" she whispered.

The walk across the gym floor to the judges' table seemed a lot farther than it looked from the bleachers, especially since my legs seemed suddenly shaky from sitting so long. It occurred to me that there may have been some advantages to being in Megan Fisher's position after all. "Uh, hi," I said breathlessly when I finally reached the table.

There were three judges: Miss Sieg, the girls' phys ed teacher, was in the center chair, while on her right sat Mrs. Hellman, the cheerleading advisor and coach of the girls' basketball team. Mr. Safranski, the football coach, was the other bookend to Miss Sieg.

"Name?" asked Miss Sieg, consulting a list on the table in front of her. The question surprised me. I'd been in Miss Sieg's gym class since freshman year, so I know she knew my name.

"Uh … L-Lucy Kellogg?" I stammered uncertainly.

"What year are you, Lucy?"

"Sophomore. Wait … I'll be a junior next year."

Miss Sieg wrote something on her list and looked up at me. I wished she'd crack a smile or something, but her face was carefully neutral. "All right, Lucy," she said. "Whenever you're ready."

"Should I … um, any particular order?" I didn't want to screw anything up.

"Just however you like, dear." Both she and Mrs. Hellman smiled at me now, but Mr. Safranski looked bored and was playing with his pen.

"All right." I backed away from the table and took a deep breath, then wound up for my jumps. *Herkie … split jump … arch jump … pike …* The adrenaline pumped through my veins and the yellow lights of the gym made everything feel dreamlike. On the other hand, I felt exhilarated. I was nailing the jumps, and I imagined that the crowd had fallen into a respectful silence.

I was just winding up for my specialty, a toe touch so lofty and flawless that they'd never forget me, when all of a sudden a loud noise came from somewhere outside the auditorium. It wasn't important whether it was a car backfiring or an atomic bomb detonating—what mattered was that it startled me and threw me off balance, causing what had started out as a perfect toe touch to fizzle into a pathetic version of a jumping jack. To make matters worse, I landed on the backs of my heels, windmilling my arms like a tap dancer doing the butterfly as I fell down, down …

"Aww-w-w," moaned the crowd as I continued backwards in slow motion. The drama of my aborted jump had definitely reclaimed their interest. "Ooooooh," they chorused a second later, when my butt hit the gym floor. A lightning bolt of pain flashed through my tailbone and shot up my back. I opened my mouth and hollered *something*, but you can bet it wasn't "Rah!" or "Go team!" In the next instant, I was teetering on the brink between shock and tears, not sure which way I'd go.

A single cry of "Oh *no*, Lucy!" rang through the air, spoken in a voice that sounded suspiciously like Rachel's. *Lucy... Lucy... Lucy,* the crowd murmured in a low buzz. If I'd wanted to become better known at my school, this was definitely a step in the right direction.

For an instant after I landed, I was too stunned to move, and by the time I'd recovered, the judges had all gotten to their feet and were leaning over the table looking down at me. "Are you all right, Lucy?" Mrs. Hellman asked with concern. Mr. Safranski had dropped his pen and was coming around to help me to my feet.

"I'm fine... really," I assured them, waving Mr. Safranski away and getting to my feet as nimbly as my sore tailbone would allow.

"Would you like to try that one again?" Miss Sieg offered. I considered it, but at that point it was all I could do to stand up straight.

"No," I said, shaking my head. "I don't think so."

All I wanted to do was make it back over to the bleachers and sit carefully back down. The crowd provided a sympathetic smattering of applause as accompaniment to my long walk across the gym, where Sukie's worried face greeted me.

"Holy crap, Lucy, are you okay?" she asked. "I could tell that probably hurt."

"My pride more than anything," I told her, although my tailbone was still smarting. I opened my mouth to say more, but before I could, we heard "Number thirteen!" Sukie had no choice but to leave me behind in the bleachers and take her own turn in front of the judges.

I watched as she went through the same routine as the rest of the girls, and noticed how natural she looked leaping into the air to do a perfect series of jumps. *Split jump … toe touch … herkie … pike.* Her long legs, which might have made anyone else look clumsy, actually looked graceful and gazelle-like as Sukie leapt, again and again, as if she had springs in her heels. When she was finished, the crowd (still attentive after my mishap) broke into spontaneous applause, and I heard Rachel shout, "Yay, Sukie!"

A lump rose up suddenly in my throat, but I clapped hard as Sukie nodded to the judges and loped back across the gym to her seat next to me. Her face was flushed and her eyes were shining as she sat down.

"That was so good!" I managed, finding it hard to talk with my throat closing off. "You've made it. You're going to get picked."

"I thought I'd have problems with the pike," she told me breathlessly. "But I think it went okay." She clasped my hand and we watched as the rest of the cheerleading hopefuls performed for the judges with varying degrees of success. While some of the other girls were wobbly on their landings, I couldn't help noticing that no one else actually fell on their behinds. I could only hope that the group cheer routines would go better.

"All right, ladies," Miss Sieg announced after the last girl had finished her jumps. "Now we'll go right into the group cheers." She consulted her list. "First, I'd like to see numbers four, twelve, twenty-two, twenty-four, and twenty, please."

Sukie drew in her breath and whispered, "Don't forget to smile!" I stood up stiffly and made my way out onto the floor. Now that I'd gotten up, my tailbone felt sorer than ever. I put a smile on my face anyway, determined to ignore the pain until this was all over.

Out in the middle of the gym floor, I looked around and realized that three of the four other girls surrounding me were Sarah Kenwood, Fiona Barrett, and Lauren Smith. My heart sank as I realized that three-fourths of the people I was being judged against were Perfect.

"Ready, okay!" called Fiona Barrett, the self-appointed leader of the cheer. For a split second I wondered if that would give her some kind of advantage. Then I found my arms and legs automatically trying to take up the movements of "Can't Be Beat," the cheer that everyone had learned for tryouts.

> *We are the Coyotes,*
> *We can't be beat!*
> *You Pirates watch out and prepare for defeat!*
> *We're tough, we're awesome, we're Number One!*
> *And you'll know we're the best by the time we're done!*

I tried to concentrate on making sure that my arms were straight and my voice was projecting clearly, but every movement seemed to jar my tailbone and I ended up working hardest just not to cause myself more pain. I knew that I wasn't smiling; it was all I could do to keep from grimacing.

As we finished the cheer, everyone but me went into a series of whoops and leaps; I knew better than to even attempt those kinds of acrobatics. Instead, I approached the judges table. "Hi," I said, still a little breathless from the routine. "Listen, I think maybe I did hurt my tailbone when I fell earlier, so ... I don't think I'm going to be able to keep doing the cheers."

Miss Sieg looked worried. "Maybe we should go down to the locker room so I can take a look at you."

"Oh, no." I shook my head, imagining how completely embarrassing it would be to have cheerleading tryouts interrupted so that Miss Sieg could check out my butt. "I'm fine ... " I thought fast. "In fact, my mom's up in the bleachers. I think that if I just stop jumping around I'll be fine."

The judges conferred. "All right," Miss Sieg said finally. "But I'll want to talk with your mother after tryouts are over. You may need to be seen by a doctor."

I nodded in pained agreement and headed back to the floor where the other girls were still waiting. As we turned to go back to the bleachers, Fiona Barrett asked, "Are you okay, Lucy?" I smiled weakly and nodded, surprised that she knew my name.

"Yeah, I think so," I told her, not really believing it myself.

Sukie didn't say much when I sat down, just looked at me with her gray eyes full of sympathy. I didn't even have time to explain what had happened; the judges were calling out the numbers for the next group of girls, and hers was one of them. This time Sukie ran into the center position and led off the rest of the girls in the cheer. I was proud to see Sukie take the lead role, but at the same time, something about it only added to my misery.

Sukie's group performed the cheer flawlessly, and even I could see that my best friend was undeniably one of the best. When Sukie came running back with the rest of her group, I smiled encouragingly at her but couldn't seem to come up with any words of support. It turned out I didn't need to; girls from every side were reaching out to pat her on the back and tell her how good she'd been.

After all the girls had a chance to perform as part of a group at least once, the judges called a few more groups out, this time mixing up the girls differently. I sat on the bench watching as Sukie was called out three more times with different groups. The likelihood that she was going to make one of the cheerleading squads without me was clearly increasing, and prickly tears were already gathering behind my eyes in anticipation. I wanted nothing more than to leave my seat and slip out of the gym to go home, where I'd bury myself under the slippery satin comforter on my bed and have a good sob.

Eventually, the judges were satisfied they'd seen enough, and put their heads together to tabulate the scores. When they announced the new cheer squads for the upcoming school year, Sukie's was the third name called, right after

Fiona Barrett, for the varsity squad. Everything seemed to go into slow motion as Sukie turned and hugged me, squealing, before leaping up to run out onto the middle of the gym floor. When she got there, Miss Sieg was waiting with her new orange and black WHS cheerleading jacket. I let the tears flow as I watched Fiona hug Sukie and the two of them began jumping around, clutching their jackets and sobbing with happiness. Sarah Kenwood and Lauren Smith made the JV squad, and when the rest of the positions had been announced, I was unsurprised to find myself still sitting in the bleachers along with twenty-two other disappointed girls. The crowd came streaming down from the stands to offer their congratulations to the winners, and I got gingerly to my feet to find Sukie, who had disappeared in the throng.

Just as I spotted her and was cautiously approaching the screaming, crying knot of new cheerleaders and well-wishers, Sukie looked up and saw me. "Lucy!" she cried, breaking into fresh tears as she ran across the floor towards me. The despair in her voice was real, and I felt comforted for a second. As she reached out to throw her arms around me, I took a step backwards, not wanting to invite further injury, and Sukie... laughed.

"Oops, sorry," she said, giggling. "You're still hurt."

"No problem," I told her. I knew Sukie wasn't really laughing *at* me—she was just excited and full of adrenaline—but something about it at this particular moment set my teeth on edge. We completed the hug, but now it had become a stiff, awkward thing. For an instant, our chests touched, and I could feel Sukie's heart pounding in her chest, the same way mine was.

Sukie stepped back, her happy face stained with tears. "Lucy, I never expected it to turn out like this."

"No, really, it's okay," I managed, ashamed of the way I was acting but unable to help myself. "I'm happy *you* made it at least. Hey, you did great. You deserved it." I stretched my lips in a way that I hoped was convincing.

"Congratulations, Sukie!" Mom and Rachel had found their way through the crowd and came up behind us. "Nice job!" Mom gave Sukie a hug, too, but Rachel stood quietly off to the side, looking everywhere but at me.

I sidled over and put an arm around her. "Sorry I let you down this time, kiddo," I told her. "Guess this means I'm human."

Rachel shook her head, but when she looked up at me her eyes were moist. "I wanted you to make it," she said quietly. "You would be such a great cheerleader. The best one ever."

I had to take my mind somewhere else for a second so I wouldn't start crying right there. "Oh, I don't know about that," I told her hoarsely, "Did you see me fall on my butt out there?"

Rachel smiled in spite of herself. "It could happen to anyone," she said. "I wish you could have had a do-over."

"Me too, kid. But I gotta tell ya, my butt *really* hurts … I couldn't have done one more jump no matter how much those judges begged me." I gave her a one-armed squeeze and felt her lean against me in a comforting, little-sister way.

Mom had been talking with Miss Sieg, who had come through the crowd to speak with her. "How about we swing by Urgent Care on the way home?" Mom suggested casually. "Just to make sure nothing got knocked out of place."

I glanced over to where Sukie had been standing, but she'd melted back into the crowd of well-wishers. "Whatever," I said, shrugging. "I guess I'm finished here."

Ernest Hemingway fishing in Key West in 1932.

December 4th

Lucy Dear,

You must promise me you'll travel to Key West some day just to visit Hemingway's house and see the descendants of his original cats. They're polydactyl, which means they have extra fingers and toes... wouldn't that be handy? (No pun intended, teehee!)

Remember this: I love you!

Nana Lucy

seven

The Urgent Care doctor said my tailbone was only bruised, not cracked. But for a few days the pain seemed to grow worse rather than better. I limped around school like I was harboring a stick where the sun doesn't shine, and I had to carry a pillow to sit on. All in all, the embarrassment only added to my dismal mood as I watched Sukie and the other new cheerleaders revel in their new status.

"So, I was down on first floor, and language arts is all the way up on third..." I would be complaining to Sukie, "and, well, you know how stairs are for me, so I was trying to just walk really slowly, and all of a sudden..."

"Hey, Hollister! Heard you made it! F'ing awesome!" someone would shout from across the hallway.

"Oh, thanks, Mike," Sukie would reply, waving back.

"How do you know Mike Taylor?" I'd ask, my mouth gaping after him. Mike Taylor was the hottest guy in the senior class.

Sukie would shrug. "I don't really know him... I guess somehow he just knows me."

"Huh."

"So anyway," she encouraged, "You were walking up the stairs, and..."

I couldn't tell if she was really interested or just pretending to be. "It doesn't matter," I pouted, knowing that if I continued on with my pathetic tale (my "Tail of Woe," as Mom called it), I'd only be interrupted again by another enthusiastic member of the newly formed Sukie Hollister Fan Club. In spite of my tailbone-challenged state, I'd tried to make plans with Sukie every night since tryouts, but she was always busy. Tuesday she'd had dinner with her parents to celebrate both her cheerleading and her mom's new freelance assignment, then Wednesday it was a cheerleading orientation/spaghetti feed, and Thursday she said she had to catch up on homework.

Friday was the last day of school before summer, and by then the whole thing was really beginning to get on my nerves.

"Is this how it's going to be, then?" I demanded when I arrived at Sukie's locker that morning and found her halfway inside, searching for something. Like the Hollister home, Sukie's locker was a disorganized mess.

She backed out of her locker immediately. "Is *what* 'how it's going to be'?" she asked.

"I feel like our friendship isn't even important to you anymore," I accused

The injured expression on her face made me feel slightly better. "Lucy, that's silly. Why would you even think that?"

"Well, it kind of feels that way," I sulked. "You're always busy with other stuff and don't have time to spend with me. We haven't even gotten a chance to celebrate yet."

Sukie nodded. "I know," she said. "I guess I wasn't sure you really wanted to because…well, the way things came out."

"What, so you think I'm that pathetic?" I demanded, as if I wasn't. "I've just been waiting until you were free so we could celebrate ourselves. I know how hard you worked to make it. Like I said, you deserve it."

"We both worked hard," Sukie reminded me. "We both should have made it."

Even though it didn't change things, I appreciated her saying that. "Well, anyway, I do want to celebrate."

Sukie grinned. "Great…what about tonight?" she offered. "School's finally done, so we should do something to celebrate *that* at least. We could grab a bite at the Burger Barn and then take Olive for a few laps up and down Main Street. See who's out and about, you know?"

It did sound fun. "Great plan," I said. "But it might have to be a little later. Nana Lucy is flying in after school, and we're all going out to the airport to pick her up. How about I call you after we get home?"

"Hollister!" a male voice yelled from somewhere in the passing throng of students at the same instant that Sukie's cell phone chimed the arrival of a text message. She didn't even flinch. "Okay," she said, pushing the extra refuse that was hanging out of her locker back inside and slamming the door shut. Loose papers stuck out around the edges, like the lettuce in a sandwich. She bumped her shoulder affectionately against mine as we turned to head to class. "Consider it a date."

eight

"*Flight 200 from Minneapolis is arriving at Gate One,*" came the announcement over the loudspeaker. We were at the airport waiting for Nana Lucy, and both my parents seemed unusually edgy.

"I've never understood the need to announce the gate number when there is only one gate to begin with," Dad grumbled irritably.

Out of the corner of my eye, I saw Mom give him a look. "I'm sure it's just procedure."

I didn't say anything, but moved impatiently from foot to foot like an anxious six-year-old waiting for Santa to arrive. As if the last day of school weren't exciting enough, I'd had extra butterflies in my stomach all day long, knowing that Nana Lucy was finally coming.

"There she is!" Rachel cried, jumping up and down in place. We all scanned the passengers straggling out of the gate area, and suddenly there she was. The minute I saw Nana Lucy's crisp summer blouse and tan linen skirt,

I felt infinitely better. "She looks the same," I observed, the relief evident in my voice.

"Of course she does," Mom replied, sounding a little relieved herself.

Dad was already striding the short distance to meet Nana Lucy as she came towards us, and when he reached her she held up her arms for a hug. Dad's really tall, and Nana Lucy seemed to have shrunk, so the distance between them seemed even greater than usual.

The rest of us followed, waiting our turns. "Well, look at how you've grown!" she told Michael after accepting his kiss on her cheek. "You're practically a man!"

Michael grinned self-consciously. "Yup," he agreed.

"And oh ... my Lucy!" She smiled, turning towards me with her arms outstretched. She gave me a big hug and kiss, and instantly I knew something wasn't right. Nana Lucy had always been fussy and particular about her clothes; she'd been the one to show me how to iron a collar from the ends towards the middle so as not to wind up with wrinkles at the tips. She'd always sent her and Grandpa Sam's clothes to the dry cleaners every week, rain or shine, and she washed her silk stockings out by hand so they wouldn't snag. Now, standing close to her like this, a faint odor suggested that Nana's outfit wasn't anywhere near fresh, and as I looked closer, I saw that there was a stain on the front of her blouse that suggested something spilled. I opened my mouth, but no words came out.

"They all just keep growing, Nana," Mom said, saving me from having to speak. "And yet somehow Bruce and I continue to stay as young as teenagers."

We all laughed, Nana Lucy the hardest. I couldn't help noticing that Dad's sounded a little forced, and as we made our way to baggage claim I wished I was still small enough to slip my hand into his reassuringly. Since I was too big, though, I was grateful when Rachel skipped between us and took Dad's hand.

"How long are you staying, Nana?" Rachel was asking, apparently uninformed about the reason for Nana Lucy's trip to Williston.

"Oh, probably just a few days, sweetie," Nana Lucy told her with a wink, her words colliding with Mom's quick response of "As long as we can keep her!" We all laughed again, but not as hard. I looked around for Dad's reaction, but he'd wandered away to retrieve Nana's tapestry-patterned suitcase as it traveled past on the luggage carousel.

"We're all set," he said when he'd returned with it. "The car is out in the short-term parking lot." He handed the suitcase to Michael and held out his arm to Nana Lucy, who took it primly. We all headed out through the automatic glass doors.

Outside, the day was bright. Rachel danced ahead, leaping pirouettes across the parking lot. She'd spent the winter taking figure skating classes, and had advanced three levels.

"Goodness," Nana Lucy said, squinting against the sun. "Look at her go. I remember when my feet moved like that." She turned back to look over her shoulder at me. "Did I ever tell you that I once danced with the London Ballet Company?" she asked.

"What?" This was new information to me. "You never told me that."

Dad seemed surprised too. "I don't remember hearing about it either, Mother," he admitted. "When was that?"

Nana Lucy slowed her pace, as if remembering took all of her concentration. "I'd nearly forgotten it too until I saw Rachel twirling away just now. It was when I was fourteen; my father was taking summer classes for his master's degree at the University of Colorado, and the London Ballet was in town for a special performance of *Sleeping Beauty*. They were auditioning local children for some of the extra roles, and since I'd had ballet lessons, Mother encouraged me to try out. I ended up winning the part of a fairy, and it was one of the most exciting nights of my life." Nana Lucy's eyes grew dreamy as she talked. "I'll never forget the beautiful costumes and the bright, hot stage lights. None of us were used to it, and shortly into the program one girl fainted. The other dancers carried her off the stage like it was part of the performance. For a long time after that I planned to be a ballerina when I grew up, traveling the world to dance as Aurora every night."

There was a pause while Nana reflected, and then she smiled at me. "Of course, that's not exactly what happened, is it?" she laughed. "I guess I must have forgotten all that when I met my wonderful Samuel and had our babies. Why, I haven't thought about that in years, but now that we're talking about it, I remember it like it was yesterday!"

"It sounds very glamorous," Mom said. "I never even knew that you danced."

"Oh, yes," Nana Lucy said with a laugh. "When I was much younger."

By now we were at the car, and Dad opened the back hatch so he could stow Nana's suitcase inside. "My goodness," she said when she saw that she was going to have to climb up into the Suburban. "You have to be a mountain climber to drive around these days."

"I'll help you, Nana Lucy," offered Michael. "It's not as high as it looks." With his assistance, she was up and sitting safely in the middle seat in less than a minute. Michael climbed past to sit in the third seat, and while Mom and Dad got in the front, Rachel and I settled in on either side of Nana Lucy.

"There's a stain on your blouse, Nana Lucy," Rachel said, pointing with her finger before I could signal she should shut up. "Did you spill something on it?"

Nana Lucy looked down. "Oh dear," she said, "I must have. Funny, I don't remember spilling anything."

Mom looked over the front seat. "We'll put some stain remover on it when we get home," she offered. "It looks like coffee, so it might not come out, but we can give it a try."

The rest of the way home I stared out the window, only half-listening to Nana Lucy talk about plans for the trip she still hoped to take to North Carolina. I was thinking about the night before when I'd been flipping through channels and caught a portion of a movie showing on the Classic Movie Channel. In it, a ballet troupe was dancing *Sleeping Beauty*, and one of the dancers collapsed under the hot lights. And, exactly as Nana Lucy said, the other dancers carried her offstage as if it were part of the performance.

Aunt Carol had been right: there was something wrong, and already it was becoming clear. The sensation in my stomach as the Suburban bounced along towards home was no longer butterfly wings of excitement at the prospect of Nana Lucy coming to visit. It was the fallen pieces of my broken heart, cutting into me like jagged shards of glass.

October color in Vermont.

October 10th

Dear Lucy,
    When the bus rolled across state lines into Vermont this morning, we were greeted by the sun rising on a gorgeous autumn palette of gold, red, and amber foliage.
    I've pressed the most beautiful leaf in my journal to bring back to you; I doubt the Vermonters will miss it!
    Remember this; I love you!
        Nana Lucy

LOND
PICCADILLY CIRCUS

Dear Lucy,
    Greetings

nine

When we got home, there was a message blinking for me on the answering machine. It was Frank from the AO, and he sounded frantic. "Lucy, I know that you asked not to be put on the schedule tonight," he said, his voice pleading. "But the other hostess called in sick, and since it's Friday, it's going to get crazy in here. Any chance I could get you to work for a few hours?"

I pushed the button to erase the message and thought for a minute. I'd already cleared things with my parents to go out with Sukie, and there was no way I was going to cancel out of that. Everyone from school would be out tonight, ready to kick off the summer. Too bad for Frank, I decided.

I was just reaching for the phone to call Frank with the bad news when it rang. "Hello?" I said, fully expecting it to be Sukie, wanting to finalize our plans.

"Oh ... hello, Lucy?" I recognized Mrs. Hollister's voice.

"Hi ... I mean, this is Lucy," I said, surprised to find

myself talking to Sukie's mother rather than Sukie herself. Immediately I started getting a bad vibe about our plans.

"Hi, Lucy," Mrs. Hollister said. Her voice had that amused sound, like someone had just told her a good joke. "Sukie asked me to call you, sweetie. I understand that the two of you had plans tonight, but listen, dear, the senior cheerleaders just stopped by and kidnapped her right off the couch! Apparently they're having some kind of surprise initiation tonight. Sukie didn't know a thing about it; you should have seen her face when they all came running in the front door!"

"Wow," I said, caught completely off guard by this development. Sukie hated surprises, and I could only imagine her reaction when the senior cheerleaders came tearing in the door to drag her away.

"I have no idea when, or even *if*, they'll be back tonight," Mrs. Hollister was saying. "Do you know how these initiation things work?"

"No idea," I told her. "I didn't even know they did things like that."

"Well, anyway, Lucy, Sukie mentioned that the two of you had plans tonight, so as she was heading out the door she asked me to give you a jingle and tell you she wouldn't be able to make it. I'm sorry, Lucy; I know she didn't know this was going to happen."

I tried to swallow my hurt and annoyance before it turned into full-fledged anger. "Hey, it's all right," I said, trying to sound as if I meant it. "I was just going to call her to say I got called in to work, anyway. I wouldn't have been able to make it either."

Mrs. Hollister sounded relieved. "Oh, well that's good then. At least this way no one is disappointed."

"Yeah. It *is* good," I agreed through clenched teeth.

After Mrs. Hollister assured me that she'd tell Sukie I called when ("and *if*") she returned, we hung up. I lingered by the phone for a few minutes. Normally when I felt upset I would go lie on my bed and stare at the ceiling, but Nana Lucy had gone in to lie down as soon as we'd gotten home. I didn't mind sharing my room with Nana Lucy, but at this particular moment it would have been nice to have some privacy.

Instead, I decided that now was as good a time as any to put Frank out of his misery. So I dialed the restaurant. "Adobe Oven," said an unfamiliar male voice.

"Doug?" I asked uncertainly. It would be highly unusual for the bartender to be answering the phone, and besides, it didn't really sound like him.

"Uh, no ... this is the dishwasher," came the answer. "Do you want me to get Frank? Who's this?"

I was momentarily struck dumb; the last thing I'd expected was to find myself talking directly to He Who Shall Not Be Named. "Uh, it's Lucy Kellogg," I stammered. "The hostess?"

"Oh, yeah ... hi."

"Hi." We were both silent for a beat, and I could hear Latin music and the distant clatter of restaurant noises in the background.

"So, why are you answering the phone?" I asked finally.

"The produce showed up late," he told me. "Frank's giving the deliveryman a piece of his mind. Everyone else is tied up, so when the phone rang in the kitchen, I was the only one who could grab it."

"Oh." Suddenly I remembered why I'd called. "Listen," I said, "Frank left a message asking me to come in to work tonight. Could you tell him I'll be there in a half hour?"

"Sure, I'll tell him." I might have been imagining it, but I thought I could hear a smile in his voice. To my surprise, the idea that HWSNBN would be pleased to see me caused a little flutter in my midsection. I quickly reminded myself of the nasty text message he'd sent Sukie, still clear in my mind nearly two years later.

"Okay then," I said nonchalantly. "Guess I'll see you later, then."

"Yep."

The phone went dead and I stood there staring at the receiver in my hand, wondering why I suddenly felt a little better. *Note to self: It would be unacceptable to have a crush on He Who Shall Not Be Named.* No matter how betrayed I felt by Sukie, she was still my best friend, and there were just some lines that couldn't be crossed.

At the end of the hallway, I knocked softly on my bedroom door and when I didn't hear anything, I eased it open. "Nana?" I called softly.

Nana was stretched out on my bed, her flat leather shoes sitting side by side on the floor next to it. Tiptoeing, I moved across the carpet to the closet, where I managed to open the door without a squeak and retrieve the hanger with my hostess outfit on it. I was halfway back to the door when Nana Lucy stirred and began to mutter in her sleep, freezing me in my tracks.

"It's lost, Mother," she cried suddenly. "I can't imagine where I left it! I'm so sorry!" She trailed off into murmurs, and after a few seconds I realized that she had gone back to sleep—if she'd ever been awake at all. I tiptoed the rest of the way across the room and out into the hallway, where I was closing the door softly when another voice, behind me, made me jump out of my skin.

"Hey."

I turned to find Michael standing there, his face serious. "You scared the *crap* out of me," I snapped.

Michael didn't look concerned. "Huh. Well, sorry you're so jumpy." He shrugged as if it had been my own fault.

I took a deep breath to calm myself. "Nana's talking in her sleep."

Michael half smiled; he'd grown his hair so shaggy that only the lower portion of his face was visible. "Did she say anything interesting? Reveal any scandalous family secrets?"

"Nah. I think she was dreaming about when she was a little girl. Sounds like she lost something."

Michael nodded, still looking amused. Then his face grew serious. "So...do you think they're right?" he asked me. "About Nana having Alzheimer's disease?"

"I don't know. Probably. She doesn't seem quite like the old Nana."

Michael considered this. "Or maybe she doesn't have full-blown Alzheimer's yet. Maybe it's just Half-zeimer's disease."

It took me a minute to get the joke, but then I started

laughing. "Maybe you're right," I told him. "I hope so, anyway."

"Me too."

"Well, I'd better get going." I held up my work clothes. "There's a *fuego* at the AO with my name on it."

And just maybe, the thought crept into my mind without warning, *there's something else interesting waiting for me there too.*

ten

Twenty minutes later I was on my bike riding across town to the AO. The early evening air was warm and the streets were filled with cars full of kids out celebrating the last day of school. When I stopped at the traffic light to cross Main Street, I met up with a group of guys in a white Ford Fiesta. "Show us your *tamales, señorita!*" yelled a guy my age from the driver's seat as I crossed in front of them. Main Street was the only unavoidable busy street on my way to work, but I seemed to run into a brilliant comedian every time.

"Hey, Ringling Brothers called," I retorted. "The clowns want their car back."

"Ooh," hooted the Fiesta's passengers. "Burn, sizzle, fry!" The driver scowled at me; little did he know that I'd happily trade my bike for his clown car any day of the week.

The rest of the ride was uneventful, but when I arrived at the restaurant, I saw that the AO's parking lot was already filled with cars. I quickly chained my bike to the telephone pole behind the restaurant and was heading towards the building when the back door flew open and HWSNBN came out carrying a bulging black trash bag. The front of his shirt was soaked with perspiration, dishwater, or some combination of the two. Through it, I could see the hard, flat muscles of his stomach. The sight made me slow down a little.

"Hey," he said, grunting as he hoisted the bag to throw it into the Dumpster. "You made it."

I swallowed, trying not to stare. "Uh, yeah. So, is it *muy loco* in there already?"

HWSNBN looked perplexed. "Mooey what?"

I laughed. "*Muy loco*," I translated. "Like … nuts."

He broke into a smile, and I noticed what nice teeth he had. "Oh … yeah, pretty much. Lupe's swearing like a sailor so I thought I'd come out here and give my ears a rest."

I thought about him typing "*btch*" in Sukie's text message, and wondered why a little bit of cursing from a fiery chef should bother him, but I smiled anyway. "Lupe gets a little crazy when the place is busy. If you've got virgin ears, you're not going to last long."

"Ah, I can take it." HWSNBN smiled at me, and I smiled back for a split second before I realized I was playing with serious fire and quickly rearranged my face into a neutral expression.

"Well, I guess I'd better get in there." I moved towards the door. "So … bye."

He nodded, but didn't make any move to go inside himself. "Yep, see ya," he said. "Later." I turned and walked quickly away, aware that he was watching me go. It wasn't until I was safely inside that I relaxed and started breathing again.

HWSNBN hadn't been exaggerating. It was packed inside the restaurant. "Oh, Lucy! Thank God you're here!" gasped Donna as she rushed past, carrying a tray loaded with plates of steaming food. "Frank has no idea how to balance tables. Go easy on me until those two eight-tops from hell have left, okay?"

"No problem." I hurried to the empty hostess station. Scanning the restaurant, I could see that most of the seats were filled, but Donna had several big tables while Cheryl was juggling all the smaller ones. Verona, one of the day waitresses, was working too, and was running her feet off in the side bar while Donna and Cheryl managed the big room.

A second later Frank came around the corner, looking frazzled. "Oh, thank God," he said when he saw me. I was gratified that everyone was so happy to see me. Frank grabbed a napkin off one of the tables and dabbed it at the edges of his receding hairline, where beads of sweat glistened. "I owe you big time, Lucy."

"I'll add it to your tab," I told him.

He only smiled distractedly. "I've been trying to do my best with the seating, but they're still getting pissed at me." He motioned towards Donna, who was glaring at him as she served the food to a noisy table full of women who had clearly had a few too many pitchers of Doug's extra-strength sangria.

"I can take it from here," I assured Frank. "Why don't you help them out by doing beverage refills?"

"Refills... good idea," he said, and hurried away. On his way through the big room I saw him take a detour past Cheryl. By the way she jumped when he passed behind her, I suspected he'd given her a pinch on the behind.

Rolling my eyes, I turned back to see two young couples coming through the door. "I hear this place has the best food in town," said one of the men, winking at me. "Is that true?"

"Absolutely," I told him. "Everything's awesome, but I personally recommend the *chuleta de puerco* and the *tamale* pie; they're our specials tonight." I hoped they didn't notice me reading them right off the *Especialidad* board behind them.

"Mm, it smells fantastic in here!" said one of the women, and the other one nodded in agreement. "I just love Mexican food."

"Our head chef was born and raised in Puebla, Mexico," I told her, counting out four menus. "Authentic Mexican cuisine is his specialty." I led them to a table far away from the kitchen, not wanting Lupe's sporadic but audible bouts of profanity to ruin the reputation I'd created for him. Unfortunately, this meant I had to put them in Donna's section, and I saw her shoot me a nasty look. Raising my shoulders in a gesture of apology, I headed back to greet the new batch of customers who had already come through the door.

Things didn't taper off until nearly ten o'clock, and by that time we were all ready to collapse. Donna and Verona headed outside for a quick cigarette break while Cheryl kept an eye on the last few stragglers still lingering at their tables.

With things slowing down up front, I drifted through the restaurant towards the bar area to see how Doug had weathered the storm.

He was washing glasses and looked beat. "Man, we got *slammed* tonight," he said when he saw me. "How did things go up front?"

"No problemo," I told him, blowing casually on my fingernails and then buffing them against my shoulder. "Not for a professional like me."

Doug laughed. "Are you thirsty? I could whip you up one of my special risk-free margaritas."

"Sounds great." I realized that I was parched, as Nana Lucy would say.

Doug reached up and took down one of the clean glasses he'd just hung in the overhead rack. "What's your pleasure?"

"Surprise me," I told him.

"Okay." Doug turned towards the blender. "Check back in a few minutes and I'll have it ready for you."

"Perfect."

As I headed back to the hostess station, I glanced back into the kitchen. Lupe and Julio were leaning against the prep counter drinking bottles of Dos Equis; HWSNBN was standing near the sink, stripping off his long black rubber gloves. Before I could look away he looked up; our eyes met and I felt my stomach flip over. I quickly pretended that I was looking at the clock over his head, but I knew he wasn't fooled. *Great,* I thought; when I passed the kitchen again in a few minutes, it would look like I was stalking him.

I decided to pretend I'd misunderstood Doug about coming back for the margarita. Sure enough, a few minutes later he came around the corner to the hostess station carrying my drink. "Here you go, sweet stuff." He handed me a tall, fancy glass full of a blended red beverage. He'd dipped the rim of the glass in crystallized sugar, just like a drink he'd make for a customer, and stuck a purple umbrella in next to the straw.

"Mm, strawberry," I said after I'd taken a sip. At that moment, the virgin margarita seemed like the most refreshing thing I'd ever tasted. "You are definitely my favorite bartender ever, Douglas!"

He grinned and made a little bow. "My pleasure."

As I sipped my strawberry drink slowly, to avoid getting brain freeze, Frank came back up front. "Well, I think we're in the home stretch," he told me. "You can take off whenever you're ready, Lucy." The restaurant didn't close until eleven, but once it got slow he usually let me leave. "In fact," he said, "you've been on your feet since you got here. Why don't you go sit down and enjoy that." He gestured towards the margarita.

"Excellent idea," I said gratefully.

"And, Lucy, thanks for coming in," Frank added. "I really appreciate it. From now on, I'll try to make sure you're scheduled when I know it's going to be busy."

"Okay." It wasn't like I was going to have a full social calendar, by the looks of things.

I'd just settled into a booth with my margarita when Donna and Verona came in from outside, looking like they'd both gotten a second wind.

"How was your break?" I asked, pretending to smoke an invisible cigarette. "Shave a couple more minutes off your lives?"

Verona looked around the restaurant and made a face. "If this is my life, I should probably smoke *more.*"

Donna, however, looked worried. "Lucy, did you ride your bike here tonight?"

"Mm-hm." I took a generous swig of my drink, and immediately regretted it as an ice pick of pain started to grow in my forehead. "Ugh, brain freeze...brain freeze!" I pressed my fingers to my temples as they both murmured in sympathy.

When I'd mostly recovered, Donna continued. "Listen, the reason I brought up your bike is because I know you usually chain it to that big telephone pole out in back."

I nodded. "If you're referring to my special VIP parking space, then yes, that's it all right."

"Well, when we were outside, I noticed the chain lying on the ground," she said slowly, clearly reluctant to be the bearer of bad news. "But your bike...well, it wasn't there."

The fading vestiges of my brain freeze were instantly forgotten. "Wasn't there?" I repeated, leaping out of the booth and heading for the kitchen. It was the quickest route to the back, and I didn't even give a thought to my earlier embarrassment.

"Hey, it's the hostess with the mostest!" Lupe said good-naturedly as I came hurrying into the kitchen. I gave him a vague smile and rushed towards the back, not even glancing towards HWSNBN, who was hanging Lupe's clean aluminum sauce pots back on their hooks. Throwing open the back door, I rushed outside.

As Donna had said, my bike chain was lying coiled around the bottom of the telephone pole, but my faithful blue mountain bike—the one I'd bought with birthday money when I was thirteen—was nowhere to be seen. "Shit!" I cried, running the rest of the way to the spot where my bike had been. I picked up the chain and saw that it had been cut with a neat, precise slice.

"Someone would need a saw to do that," came a voice from behind me. I turned to see that HWSNBN had followed me outside.

"I can't believe it!" I cried, furious. "How am I going to get home?" I turned the chain over in my hands, staring at it in angry disbelief. "Or anywhere?"

He came closer, and took the chain from me. "It might turn up," he said. "Maybe someone stole it for a prank. It's the last day of school and kids get a little crazy, you know? Do you have it registered in case someone finds it?"

I nodded. Dad had driven me down to the police department to fill out the papers the day I'd bought the bike.

"That's good," he said. "The police will call you then, if someone finds it and turns it in. And don't worry about getting home," he shrugged. "I've got a car here; I can give you a lift. I'm almost done in the kitchen anyway."

For a moment I was silent, trying to decide what to do or say. A moment later, I realized there was only one thing I *could* say. "Thanks," I told him wearily. "A ride would be great."

BY AIR MAIL
PAR AVION
Royal Mail

Worldwide postcard

7 000354

PHOT

The Pyramid at Night | Musée du Louvre

August 11th

Bonjour Lucille,

Greetings, Mon Cherie! Would
you believe that I'm sitting on
a bench outside the Louvre, writing this postcard to you? Paris is
absolutely breathtaking; even the
sidewalks seem elegant, somehow!
I wish so much you were here to
stroll along the Seine with moi!
Remember this: Je t'adore!
Nana Lucy

PRINTED U.S.A.

LOND
PICCADILLY CIRCUS

Dear Lucy
Greetings
land of avion
cheese? Si
the Franken
where they
gorgeous
In front of
we were
courtyard
esque; it
than though
Remem
Mo

eleven

"Well, here's the chariot," HWSNBN said, gesturing towards the old gray sedan parked on the far side of the AO's parking lot. "An '87 Bonneville."

"I'll bet you call her Bonnie, don't you?" I asked, opening the passenger door. In spite of its age, the car was neat as a pin inside and smelled of pine-tree air freshener.

He looked surprised. "How'd you know?"

"I'm psychic." I wasn't sure whether I should be more disturbed that my bike had been stolen, or to find myself riding home with He Who Shall Not Be Named. I didn't even want to *think* about Sukie's reaction if she saw me; since I didn't know exactly where the cheerleading initiation was taking place, I slumped low in my seat, just in case.

HWSNBN started the car and backed out of his spot, then pulled out of the parking lot and onto First Avenue. I didn't need to look back to know that Donna and the other waitresses were probably watching out the window, high-fiving each other as we drove away.

"So, where are we headed?" he asked finally, and I realized I hadn't even told him where I lived.

"Oh, sorry," I said, "It's 1218 Chess Drive."

"Ah, Snob Hill," HWSNBN said, smiling.

"It's at the *foot* of Snob Hill," I told him. "My friend, Sukie Hollister..." I stopped abruptly. I'd been about to tell him that Sukie actually lived on Snob Hill, but I suddenly remembered who I was talking to.

"Sukie Hollister?" he repeated. "That girl who drives the green Volkswagen?"

I paused for a beat. "Yeah," I said finally. "That's Sukie. She's my best friend." I figured this was as good a time as any to point out where my loyalties lay.

HWSNBN drove silently for a moment, then glanced at me as he looked over his shoulder to change lanes. "That girl hates me, for some reason," he said. "I didn't know she was your best friend."

I decided to play innocent. "What makes you think she hates you?"

He shook his head. "She always gives me the snake eye at school, and one time when I bumped into her in the hallway she called me an a-hole. I don't get it, because when I first met her, she seemed cool." He glanced over at me. "Hey, if you're her best friend, you probably know all about it."

I shrugged noncommittally, not sure how much Sukie would want me to say. To be safe, I decided to change the subject. "So, who do you hang out with?" I asked.

He considered. "Lots of different people. Mostly Cody

Griffin and Connor Burmeister. I used to hang some with Tyler Driscoll until he moved away last year."

I had heard that Tyler's family had moved to Florida, but I didn't say anything, since the mention of Tyler brought us right back to that painful afternoon when Sukie and I were talking about setting me up with Tyler. Just before she got the kiss-off text from HWSNBN. "Uh, didn't you used to date Sarah Kenwood?" I asked, now that I was reminded of everything.

He looked surprised. "We went out a few times freshman year, but that was it. I'm not really with anybody right now," he added, glancing at me again. I felt myself blush; I certainly didn't want him to think I was asking if he had a girlfriend for any particular reason.

"How about you?" he asked. "Are you seeing anybody?" Unlike me, HWSNBN didn't seem at all concerned about what impression his questions might be giving.

"No," I answered. "I keep pretty busy with work and … other stuff."

He didn't say anything, and silence filled the car for the rest of the drive to my house.

"Well um, anyway … thanks for the ride," I said, reaching for the door handle. "I really appreciate it." I could see that a light was still on in the family room and my mind had already jumped five minutes ahead, when I would be inside telling my family the traumatic story about my stolen bike.

"Uh, hey … wait a sec." HWSNBN reached his hand out to stop me as I started to get out. At the touch of his warm fingers, I felt the fine hairs along my arm rise, which made me shiver involuntarily. I saw that he looked nervous, suddenly. It was the first time I'd looked at him directly since the day I'd officially met him in the AO kitchen, and in the dim yellow haze of the ancient dome light, I noticed that his eyes weren't green, but hazel, and that his eyelashes were as thick as fringe.

HWSNBN hesitated. "I was thinking that...well... maybe we should hang out together sometime. Not at work, I mean," he finished awkwardly.

I froze, one foot in the car, the other outside on the safe, firm ground. In a flash I thought about how much fun it might be to go out on a real date—to sit next to him in a movie and feel my stomach flip over when he took my hand; to wonder whether he was going to kiss me at the end of the night. The romantic montage playing in my mind came to a sudden screeching halt, however, replaced by the image of Sukie's betrayed, devastated face when I told her I was going to go on a date with He Who Shall Not Be Named, the guy who'd called her a bitch and implied that she was ugly.

I forced myself to look up and meet his eyes so there would be no misunderstanding of what I meant. "I don't think that would be a very good idea," I told him as straight-out as I could. "But thanks for the ride...really."

HWSNBN didn't say anything, but the light in his eyes faded a little and there was nothing left to do but get the rest of the way out of the car and shut the door. I heard him put Bonnie into gear, and he pulled away, leaving me standing on the curb.

As I walked up the driveway into the house, I noticed

that although the light was on in the family room, the rest of the house was dark. I'd probably missed my chance for any sympathy that night. It didn't matter, though. At this point, I probably needed sympathy for more than just a stolen bike.

twelve

When I got inside, things were as quiet as I'd suspected; everyone had gone to bed. I was suddenly starving, so I decided to make myself a snack. I'd just located a package of Oreos that Mom had hidden in the back of the cupboard when a noise from the hallway almost made me drop them.

"My, the sky is certainly dark this morning. Are we expecting a storm?" Nana Lucy asked from the doorway. I turned to look at her, and immediately noticed that something was wrong. Despite the fact that it was nearly midnight, she was wearing a flowered silk blouse and tailored blue skirt. Her handbag was on her arm, and she looked ready for an event of some kind.

"Oh, Nana, it's you! I thought everyone had gone to bed." The nap she had earlier must be keeping her up, I thought.

"Of course, dear," Nana assured me. "I slept like a baby, but I didn't want to miss church!" She glanced around the empty kitchen. "Isn't anyone else going besides the two of us?" she asked.

I stared at her for a second before I realized what she meant. "Nana," I told her gently, "it's almost midnight, not morning." I pointed to the clock over the sink, which said 11:47 p.m. "Everyone's in bed. And besides," I added, "tomorrow is Saturday, not Sunday."

In my chest, my heart was fluttering like a moth. Could things with Nana Lucy really be this bad?

A look of confusion crossed Nana Lucy's face. "Saturday?" she said faintly. "Oh dear ... I must have gotten my days mixed up again." She set her purse down on the kitchen table and looked so discouraged that I set the package of cookies on the counter and hurried over to help her into a chair, feeling sick about things.

"Oh, for goodness' sake, I'm not an invalid." She waved me way. "Please don't treat me like one." There was a measure of annoyance in her voice that I'd never heard before, and I backed away immediately to let her find her seat on her own. It wasn't like Nana Lucy to be snappish with anyone, least of all me, but I knew she was upset with herself so I tried not to take it personally.

"Oh, Lucy, I'm sorry," she sighed when she was settled. "Bring me one of those cookies, won't you?"

I figured we could both use some, so I hurried to get the Oreos and pour us each a cold glass of milk. "It could probably happen to anyone, Nana Lucy," I told her, sitting down across from her. "You had that nap earlier, and you got mixed up."

Nana Lucy snorted. "Mixed up," she repeated. "Mixed

up, confused, crazy; what's the difference? The point we keep coming back to is that I seem to be losing my mind, just like your Aunt Carol says."

"No, Nana," I told her, trying to be reassuring. "Listen ... don't say that. You're not losing your mind."

Nana Lucy twisted the top off her cookie and stared at the white filling as if it held the answer to her problems. "What if I am?" she said finally. "My mother had Alzheimer's. By the time she died, she didn't even know her own children."

I was silent, glad that I'd taken a bite of cookie so I didn't have to respond. I wanted to tell her that she wouldn't end up that way, but the truth was, she was probably right.

Nana Lucy sighed, then replaced the top of her cookie and took a bite. "Well, these are still delicious, no matter how addle-brained I become."

I laughed in spite of myself, keeping my hand over my mouth so I wouldn't blow cookie crumbs out onto the table.

"So how's your life, Lucy-girl?" she asked. Then she stifled a smile. "Your mother told me that the cheerleading tryouts didn't go too well."

I snorted. "That's an understatement. I made a complete idiot of myself."

"Well, you're in good company," Nana said, making a wry face. She reached for her glass of milk. "If I *do* say so myself."

"Even if I didn't make any of the cheerleading squads," I continued, "at least Sukie made it. We were going to do something together tonight to celebrate the end of school, but she ended up having a cheerleading thing she had to go to at the last minute. So I decided to go to work instead."

Nana Lucy set down her milk glass and regarded me. "Guess I might feel bad if my best friend was all caught up in something that I couldn't be a part of."

I shook my head. "No, I'm happy for her." I hoped that if I just kept saying it, it might eventually feel true. "It's just that ... well, I hope it's not going to keep coming between us. By taking up too much of her time, I mean."

"It might." That was one thing about Nana Lucy; she was never one to beat around the bush just to make a person feel better.

"Oh, and guess what? Someone stole my bike tonight," I suddenly remembered to report. "It was chained up behind the restaurant as usual, and when I came out ... gone-zo."

"Oh, dear. How did you get home?"

I told her about HWSNBN giving me a ride home in Bonnie, and about his asking me if I wanted to hang out with him sometime. "And what did you say?" she asked, smiling.

"I told him that I didn't think it was a good idea."

Nana Lucy looked surprised. "But isn't 'hanging out' the same thing as asking you on a date?"

"Yeah, it's kind of the same thing. Except we say things like 'get some dinner' and 'see a movie' instead of 'go on a date.'"

She nodded. "I see. So this boy asked you to 'hang out,' and you told him you didn't want to. Don't you like him?"

"Well, there's more to the situation. There's like ... *history*."

"Ah, *history*." Nana nodded, as if she knew all about it. "The boy broke the girl's heart in a previous life?"

"No, the boy broke the girl's *best friend's* heart."

Nana raised her eyebrows. "I see your problem. And this young fellow knows the reasons behind your rejecting his invitation?"

"I'm not sure," I admitted. "He knows that she hates him, that's for sure. But I kind of got the impression tonight that he might not know the reason."

"Hmm, but you decided to punish him anyway."

I gestured helplessly. "She's my best friend, Nana. I saw how hurt she was."

Nana smiled. "And how does your best friend feel about you working with the cad?"

"First of all, I don't 'work with him'; he's in the kitchen and I'm in the front. And second of all, um ... I haven't exactly told her that he works there yet."

Nana Lucy didn't say anything for a second and my words hung in the air between us, along with the obvious question. Finally I couldn't take it anymore. "I don't *know* why I haven't told her yet!" I sputtered. "It just never seems like the right time. First, cheerleading tryouts were coming up, and then Sukie made it and she was so excited and it didn't seem like a good time to tell her, and ever since then we've both been so busy ... "

I stopped babbling and took a breath. Nana dunked a second cookie into her milk and took a thoughtful bite.

"You're a good friend, I'm sure," she said. "You'll tell her about it when it's the right time."

I thought about that. "Yeah," I said, hoping she was right.

"And speaking of 'the right time,'" Nana continued, glancing down at her blouse, "I think I'll go change into my nightgown, if you could kindly confirm for me that it is, indeed, appropriate attire for the occasion."

I smiled. "I think that should be fine." She disappeared down the hallway, and a few minutes later was back, holding up one of Serena's old prom dresses from my closet. "How about this for breakfast attire?" she suggested.

"They'll have you in the loony bin by lunchtime," I predicted.

Nana winked. "Might be worth it." Chuckling, she headed off to bed.

I rinsed out our glasses and put them in the dishwasher, then wiped the crumbs off the table. I was more worried about Nana Lucy than ever, but at the same time I felt better in some ways. Sure, she was a little confused once in a while, but it still seemed like there might be other possible explanations than that she was losing her marbles. And a person who really had Alzheimer's wouldn't be able to joke about it, would they? Or was I only holding onto a faint hope?

Also on my mind was HWSNBN and the nervousness in his voice when he asked if I wanted to get together sometime. Just thinking about the way his voice cracked when he suggested it made me feel oddly light-headed. And now we'd both be uncomfortable when we saw each other at work. The more I thought about it, the more I felt like I really should have given him a better explanation. After all, aside from what he'd done to Sukie, I didn't have anything against him personally. He actually seemed pretty cool; it was becoming harder for me to reconcile the HWSNBN I knew from the AO with the one who'd treated Sukie so coldly.

More importantly, I knew now that I had to let Sukie in on the situation. Maybe the passage of time and her exciting new life as a cheerleader would make her see how long ago it had all happened, and how unimportant it was in the grand scheme of things. And if everything went better than I expected, who knew? Maybe I'd take HWSNBN up on his offer to hang out sometime. A person just never knew what was going to happen.

I certainly didn't.

Worldwide
postcard

Steven Spielberg and Roy Scheider during the filming of Jaws.

February 22nd

Dearest Lucy,

Our group enjoyed a tour of
Universal Studios this morning,
the highlight of which was an unexpected encounter with that terrible
shark from the Jaws movie. It was
so enormous and frightening that
I might consider retiring my swimming
suit!

Remember this: I love you!

Nana

P.S. I hope you can read my writing;
I'm still trembling with fear!

PHOT

LONDO

PICCADILLY CIRCUS

Dear Lucy

thirteen

As much as I wanted to convince myself that Nana Lucy's memory problems were just a big misunderstanding, by the following week it became impossible to deny that there was something really wrong with my grandmother.

"Honestly, I'm afraid to leave her alone," Mom said, after she'd found a carton of vanilla ice cream in the kitchen cupboard. She was attempting to sop up the slimy mess with a dish towel, and glanced over her shoulder to make sure that Nana Lucy was still watching television in the family room. That was another thing; Nana Lucy seemed to suddenly have developed an avid interest in television, something she'd never had much time for in the past. Mostly she watched old movies on AMC, with the occasional break for *Totally Raven* or *The CBS Nightly News* when Rachel or Dad insisted. She especially seemed to like movies made by a fat director called Alfred Hitchcock, or ones in which a google-eyed actress named Bette Davis went about all sorts of mean business, including murder. I wasn't a bit surprised the day Mom found a kitchen knife buried in Nana Lucy's laundry basket.

"It's all those scary movies she watches," I told her. "I think it makes her nervous."

"Well it's making me nervous, too." Mom showed the knife to Dad, and after that they made sure Nana Lucy mostly watched comedies starring Lucille Ball or Jimmy Stewart.

Other times, Nana Lucy seemed completely like her old self, beating Michael at backgammon until he scowled and demanded they play something else, and telling Rachel stories about her travels to Europe and Japan. "The people of Japan are the most polite I've ever met," she told us. "The rest of the world could learn something from them. They do everything possible to avoid conflict."

"What about World War II?" Dad baited her from across the room, where he was reading the newspaper in his favorite chair. "How did they get involved in that?"

"You can bet it wasn't their idea," Nana Lucy retorted.

Dad loves to debate historical politics, so I was surprised when he didn't come back with some piece of information suggesting that the Japanese had, indeed, been single-handedly responsible for WWII. Instead, he changed the subject by asking Rachel to go see what Mom was making for dinner.

Nana Lucy must have been surprised, too, because a moment later she got up and commented quietly that she thought she'd check the garden for early tomatoes to have with dinner. The late-afternoon sun had slipped behind a cloud and I knew Mom would want her to put on a sweater; but I figured that if I suggested it, Nana might take it the wrong way. So I said nothing. She'd made it clear that she didn't appreciate being treated like a child.

Twenty minutes later, when Mom called us for dinner, Nana Lucy still hadn't come back inside. "Could you go out and find her, Lucy?" Mom asked. "I looked out the window but I can't see her anywhere. She must be somewhere around the side of the house, or maybe in the front yard."

Outside, the sun hadn't reappeared, and the air was growing chilly. When I looked up, I saw that the sky was turning the grayish purple that usually signals an approaching rainstorm.

"Nana?" I called, walking around the east side of the house where Mom's petunia beds were already blooming in vivid pinks and fuchsias. When I didn't see her anywhere, I circled through the back yard and around the other side of the house, but there was no sign of her. Before I let myself get nervous, I made a second circuit around in case I'd somehow missed her, but when I still didn't find her I went back into the garage and stuck my head inside the back door.

"She's not out here," I called to Mom, who was standing by the kitchen counter tossing a salad to go with the spaghetti she'd made. "I've looked everywhere."

Mom's face grew worried. "You don't suppose she'd just wander off on her own without telling us?" When I had no answer, she called out, "Bruce! Your mother seems to have disappeared. Can you go outside and help Lucy look for her?"

I cast a longing look across the kitchen at the steaming

bowl of spaghetti already cooling on the table, then resignedly went back outside to wait for Dad. *Why did Nana have to pick dinnertime to disappear?* I thought.

When Dad came out, Michael was with him. "I'm sure she just went for a little walk," Dad said. "How far could she have gotten?"

Michael and I nodded in agreement and the three of us set off down the driveway. When we got to the bottom, Dad paused. "I'm thinking maybe we should split up." He gestured up the sidewalk. "I'll go this way and the two of you head the other way, towards Spring Lake Park."

It seemed like a reasonable plan, so Michael and I set off to the east while Dad moved away from us in the other direction. After a few minutes, I felt a raindrop land on my head. "Man, we should have brought an umbrella," said Michael, reading my mind. "Now we're all going to get soaked." Before I could answer him, raindrops as fat and warm as tears were plopping onto our heads and spattering the sidewalk below.

Michael and I continued along, side by side, our heads bent against the rain. Soon my T-shirt was soaked and my hair had plastered itself to my head. Rain always makes my skin itch, but I knew we couldn't turn back until we'd found her.

Suddenly, Michael lifted his hand and pointed. "There's Nana." I followed the direction of his finger and at first I didn't see anything, but then there she was, sitting at a picnic table in the middle of Spring Lake Park, partially sheltered by the branches of an elm tree.

"Doesn't she know it's not safe to sit under a tree in a

thunderstorm?" I asked Michael as we hurried towards her through the wet grass. "Why didn't she just come home?"

Nana Lucy looked up as we neared her, and the frightened look in her eyes told me everything I needed to know. "Oh my heavens, I'm so glad to see you children!" she cried. "I was just going to go for a little walk to stretch my legs, and the next thing I knew, I'd lost my way."

I didn't see any point in reminding her that she'd left the house only intending to hunt through Mom's garden for tomatoes. Like Michael and me, Nana Lucy was soaked to the skin and shivering. With her clothing slicked against her body, I could see how thin she was. "Let's go home," I told her, as Michael helped her to her feet.

"Do you two know the way?" she asked in a voice so small and plaintive that a sudden lump grew in my throat.

"Yes, Nana," I told her hoarsely, trying to make my voice as gentle and reassuring as possible. "We know exactly how to get there." She let me take her hand, and together the three of us hurried through the park towards home.

Dad arrived home a few minutes after we did, worried sick. His face registered stark relief when he saw Nana Lucy sitting in a chair in the kitchen, wrapped in damp towels that Mom replaced with fresh, dry ones while she ran a warm bath for her.

"Mother, I'm so glad you're safe!" Dad exclaimed, coming across the kitchen floor to give her a hug without even stopping to take off his soggy shoes. I thought Mom would freak out when she came back and saw the wet footprints he'd left, but she didn't even seem to notice. Dad seemed smaller, somehow, with his hair plastered down from the rain and the rattled-but-relieved look on his face; I wondered if Mom just didn't have the heart to get on his case about wet shoes.

"Your bath is ready, Nana," Mom said. Her tone was upbeat but her face was blotchy, as if she'd been crying. "I put a fresh nightgown and robe in the bathroom for you to put on afterwards. Why don't Lucy and I help you get settled in there?"

I had already changed out of my wet things and was just putting a plate of spaghetti in the microwave for reheating, but I changed direction and went to help Mom. Nana seemed to have trouble straightening up at first, as if the cold had crept into her bones, but once she got moving, she seemed to grow looser.

"I can make it," she said, shaking us off. "Thank you, Margo, for drawing the bath for me. I'm sure it will be lovely."

Mom and I watched uncertainly as she made her way down the hallway to the bathroom. She went inside and closed the door.

Mom turned to Dad, her eyes beseeching. "Bruce, we've got to do something. The kids said she wandered all the way down to the park and couldn't find her way back. What if something terrible had happened? If she'd been hit by a car or something..."

"I know." Dad shook his head. "You can't imagine the thoughts I was having when I was looking for her. You hear about these things happening on the news all the time; an elderly person gets confused and just wanders away..."

"I think Carol's right about the evaluation," Mom

said. "It's important to get to the bottom of all this as soon as possible. If she's got Alzheimer's, at least we'll know what we're dealing with. And maybe there's some kind of treatment available."

Dad sighed, his expression grim. Finally, he nodded. "You're right. We need to sit down with her tonight and make a plan while all of this is still fresh in her mind. Maybe she'll be open to having an evaluation, especially if there's a possibility of some sort of treatment."

Mom looked relieved. She hesitated a moment, then spoke in a quiet voice. "I was talking to Barb Spicer the other day, and she said that there's a specialist in Minot who evaluates memory problems. It's a two hour drive, but..."

Dad shrugged. "I guess the distance doesn't matter," he said. "I'll call tomorrow and make an appointment."

So it was settled. The evaluation was going to happen. And when my parents talked to Nana Lucy later that night, she readily agreed to let them drive her to Minot to see the memory specialist. Everyone seemed to relax after that.

But later, I lay on the other side of the queen-sized bed with a lump in my throat, listening to my grandmother weep quietly into her pillow.

fourteen

"If you see a mighty Coyote, then you'd better step aside..."

I listened to Sukie mutter yet another cheer under her breath as she spooned peanut butter cookie dough onto a baking sheet. In the three weeks since school had let out it had been difficult to find time to spend together, between cheerleading practice and my hours at the AO. So, today, we'd come to Sukie's house to make a batch of cookies.

I dipped a fork into sugar and pressed it down onto the plump, golden ball of dough, then cleared my throat pointedly. Sukie looked up with an apologetic expression on her face. "Sorry, was I doing it again?"

I nodded. "I'm starting to think I should talk to your parents about hiring a deprogrammer." The truth was, I was both fascinated and envious to hear all the things she had to tell about her life as a new cheerleader, from the embarrassing initiation antics ("they made us do all our jumps on the island in the middle of Main Street!" Sukie had confessed, her face red but thrilled at the memory; "everyone was honking! I felt like such an idiot!") to the early morning practices ("eight o'clock every day! In the *summer!* Doesn't that suck?") to the friendships she was making that didn't include me.

"And you know those girls we used to call 'the perfect people'? Well, it turns out they're not so bad after all," Sukie confided. "In fact, Fiona had us all over to her house for lunch last Wednesday after practice, and I even talked to Sarah Kenwood. She's not my favorite person, but she's okay."

It was the perfect opportunity for me to bring up He Who Shall Not Be Named, and tell Sukie that I saw him nearly every day at the AO. On the other hand, I was feeling a little guilty. After he had given me a ride home and I'd turned him down flat, he'd avoided me, and I was surprised to find that it actually bothered me. After three days of this, I started making up reasons to stop by the kitchen; eventually HWSNBN stopped turning his back when I came in. Now we were scheduling our breaks to coincide with each other's, and generally spent them hanging around outside the back door, sipping icy Cokes that Doug served up in frosted glasses. One topic that somehow never came up, however, was my friendship with Sukie and her history with him. I'm not sure if I was the one not talking about it, or whether HWSNBN was leaving it alone. We seemed to talk about everything else under the sun except that.

So maybe it was because I knew it had just gone on too long to confess the whole thing now, or maybe because I felt envious of Sukie's life, where new, exciting things were happening. But for whatever reason, I said nothing, and the moment passed. Sukie dropped the last spoonful of dough onto the cookie sheet and I put my fork imprint on it, then watched her slide the cookies into the oven. While I rinsed out the bowl, Sukie put away the rest of the supplies, and then we sat down to wait.

As the delicious aroma of peanut butter began to fill the kitchen, Sukie asked about Nana Lucy. "It's weird," I told her. "Sometimes she still seems so normal that I think we're all making a big deal out of nothing, but the next minute she'll do something weird like try to put her pantyhose on over her house slippers. Last week she wore the same clothes for three days in a row before Mom talked her into changing."

I filled Sukie in on a few more of Nana Lucy's greatest hits, but I felt funny talking about her that way. I knew the old Nana Lucy would be sad and embarrassed about the new one.

Sukie shook her head and sighed. "Isn't there anything they can do?"

I shook my head. "Mom and Dad are taking her to Minot to see a specialist on Wednesday," I told her. "If it's really Alzheimer's, there are medications to slow it down. But it might not even *be* Alzheimer's; the nurse told Dad there are lots of other things that can cause memory problems in older people."

"Really? Like what?"

I tried to remember everything Dad had told me. Since Nana Lucy had arrived, my parents had been treating me more like a grown-up, the way they'd acted towards Serena before she left for college. Although it was sometimes hard to handle the information they shared with me, it felt good, too.

"Oh, like depression," I told Sukie now. "And sometimes I do think Nana Lucy is depressed. She cries at night when she thinks I'm asleep."

Sukie poked at a pebble of dough that had escaped from the bowl. "I'm sure I'd cry, too, if I was losing myself like that."

"Yeah." I thought of something else. "The nurse also told Dad that medication can cause confusion in people Nana Lucy's age, but she's not really on any medication. She also said that sometimes an older person's body chemistry can get out of whack, and then it's just a matter of figuring out how to correct it."

Sukie considered. "Well, maybe it's just something like that," she said optimistically. "Do you ever feel, you know... *scared* sleeping with her in the same room? I mean, how can you know for sure what she'll do?"

I thought about it. In all honesty, I never felt worried that Nana Lucy would endanger anyone but herself. "No, not really," I said. "She's still the same person; she just gets confused sometimes. It's worse when she's tired." Come to think of it, I'd recently started waking up during the night to discover that Nana Lucy had gotten out of bed, leaving a warm hollow beside me where she'd been. I'd assumed she'd gone to use the bathroom; by the time I woke up in the morning, she was back where she belonged, snoring softly on the next pillow. I made a mental note to mention it to Dad.

"I'm just hoping this can get all figured out and she

can get back to normal," I said. "Aunt Carol called Dad and asked if she should start cleaning out Nana Lucy's apartment, but he told her to wait. I think he's hoping she'll still be able to go back there. We all are," I added. It had been kind of nice having Nana Lucy with us, but it wasn't exactly the entertaining, carefree visit we were all used to.

"Man, I'd be mad if my kids got rid of all my stuff without telling me," Sukie said. I nodded.

"Me too."

A few minutes later the timer on the oven sounded, and Sukie pulled on silvery quilted oven mitts and took out the tray of cookies. "Oh my God, they smell fantastic!" I said, leaning over to inhale the warm, rich aroma.

Sukie got a plate from the cupboard and we loaded it up with cookies, yelping as we burned our fingers. While we waited impatiently for the cookies to cool enough so we could eat them, Sukie poured us glasses of cold milk.

"You know," I said, taking a sip, "my parents are leaving tomorrow morning for the drive to Minot, for the appointment, and Rachel's going with them. Michael's away at soccer camp, so basically..."

"...you've got the house to yourself," Sukie finished, grinning. "Sounds like a perfect opportunity for one of our famous sleepovers!"

"Yep. Unless you've got a cheerleading thing." Tomorrow was Tuesday, so it seemed unlikely that she would have anything important, but Sukie hesitated, thinking for a moment. To tell you the truth, it was almost long enough to make me want to rescind my offer.

"Nope," she said finally. "But I do have practice the next morning at eight, so I'll have to make sure to set the alarm. I can't oversleep and miss it."

I nodded and reached for a cookie. "Of course not." The cookie was heavy and moist, and I had an impulsive urge to crumple it into an oily ball in my fist. Instead, I took a careful, controlled bite.

"Well, listen," I told her when I'd swallowed. "I have to work the dinner rush at the AO tomorrow, but I should be home by seven thirty. Why don't you plan to come by around eight?" Since he was away at camp, I'd been using Michael's bike to get back and forth to work.

"Sure." Sukie reached for another hot cookie. It was so fresh that fractures immediately began to appear in its golden surface, and a heavy piece broke away to fall on the table with a soft *thunk*. She scooped it up and popped it in her mouth. "I'll be there with bells on," she said with her mouth full.

Just as long as you leave your pom-poms at home, I thought to myself.

Mt. Rushmore near completion in 1940.

May 30th

My Dearest Lucy,

   As you can see from the picture on the front, I'm writing this from beautiful Mt. Rushmore. Your Grandpa Sam and I honeymooned here in the Black Hills, and it's every bit as breathtaking as it was back then. Tomorrow morning we're off to Deadwood to pan for gold; let's hope I strike it rich!

   Remember this: I love you!
   Nana Lucy

P.S. George, Thomas, Teddy and Abe send their best!

LOND

PICCADILLY CIRCUS

fifteen

"We'll be back by dinnertime tomorrow, at the very latest," Mom told me. "It depends on how things go." Nana Lucy's appointment was at 8:30 a.m. sharp, which was why they were leaving today to drive the 120 miles to Minot. "Dr. Thompson's office said that she'd be in testing most of the day."

"Will she be in any pain?" I was looking forward to having the house to myself, but knowing that my grandmother was undergoing an uncomfortable procedure would certainly take the fun out of it.

"Oh no," Mom assured me. "There's no pain whatsoever. They said it's kind of like puzzles and games, and she'll be working with Dr. Thompson's technician, Tonja. They call it testing, but it's like a hearing test, not the kind of thing you can fail."

"Then what does it tell?"

"It tells how her brain is working, how the different parts of it are working. And hopefully it will tell us about what's causing her to get so mixed up."

"Huh." I did feel reassured after hearing Mom describe what Nana Lucy was getting into. Puzzles and games didn't sound very terrible.

"So you'll be all right home alone here?" Mom sounded apprehensive herself.

"Of course, Mom; I'm sixteen. Or, as some would say, 'old enough to drive,'" I couldn't resist adding. "And besides, Sukie's sleeping over so I won't really be alone."

"Well, I know. Just make sure the doors are locked before you go to bed, okay?"

I smiled patiently and made a criss-cross motion over my heart with my finger. "I promise."

"Let's get this show on the road," Dad said, coming into the kitchen with Nana Lucy's overnight bag. It looked like a purse in his big hand, but I knew better than to laugh. Dad's sense of humor had always been a little limited, and I figured that would be even more the case now.

"I'm almost packed. Just let me grab a different pair of shoes." Mom hurried out of the room, and Dad came over to drop a goodbye kiss on my head.

"I trust that your mother laid down the law," he chided. "No boys, no wild parties, no non-domesticated animals in the house..."

"Got it, Dad. Sukie's spending the night."

Dad frowned, pretending to look stern. "Didn't I just say, 'no wild parties'?"

"Very funny." It was lame, but I appreciated the effort.

Nana Lucy came into the kitchen, looking rattled. "Oh, Bruce, thank heavens you found my bag. I've looked everywhere for it."

"Mother…" he reminded her patiently, "I told you I was taking it out to the car."

"Well then, I must not have heard you." Nana sniffed. She had dark circles under her eyes; I knew firsthand that she'd tossed and turned most of the previous night. In fact, I was looking forward to everyone leaving so that I could catch up on some of the sleep I'd missed lying next to her. I loved Nana, but I didn't love being her bed partner; it was like sleeping with a hyperactive seal.

"Let's go, let's go!" sang Rachel, bopping into the kitchen. "I want to go!" She was untangling the cord of her iPod, and I knew that she'd be lost in her own world for most of the trip.

"Well, since you're driving, we couldn't leave without you," Dad joked. I began to wonder whether my dad was one of those people who *only* had a sense of humor in crisis situations.

"Da-a-ad!" Rachel giggled at the absurdity of the idea.

Nana Lucy's eyes grew wide. "Bruce, that child's far too young to drive," she told him. "I'm sure it's … well, it's probably illegal!"

"He's just kidding, Nana," I said. Even this was new; the old Nana Lucy was usually the one cracking the jokes, or at least she was in on them.

Nana Lucy looked uncertain. "Well, I should think so."

Twenty hectic minutes later they were in the car and I was standing in the driveway, bidding them goodbye. "Good luck, Nana," I said before I closed the door.

"Yeah, like *luck's* going to have anything to do with it," she replied wryly.

I couldn't help but smile, and then they were off and I had the house to myself. It didn't take me long to end up back under the covers, luxuriating in the feeling of having my bed all to myself again.

I fell back asleep with the birds chirping outside my window, and didn't wake up until early afternoon ... floating regretfully to the surface of a dream in which I was lying on a silky, lavender flower blossom drifting lazily down a gently flowing stream.

When I was fully awake, I realized with a start that I'd slept through Scooby's regular walk time. Sure enough, when I came out into the kitchen, he was waiting by the back door with an expression of extreme doggy urgency on his face. "Good boy, Scooby," I told him after I'd glanced around for puddles and found none. "Thanks for waiting." I opened the door and followed him outside, then waited while he did his business against a tree beside the garage. Dad usually liked us to take him for an actual walk, but I was still in a lazy mood and didn't feel like venturing far.

When we got back inside, I checked to make sure Scooby had food and water, then took a long hot shower. It was still too early to get changed for work, so I flipped on the television. It was set on the Classic Movie channel, of course, and I watched for a while. The movie was about a man who'd dropped in on his sweet old aunts, only to discover that they were actually serial murderers who kill lonely old men. All of the actors were vaguely familiar, and

I knew Nana Lucy had probably told me their names at one point or another, but I couldn't remember any of them. I hoped it wasn't a sign that I'd eventually get Alzheimer's myself.

Just as I was feeling grateful that Nana Lucy wasn't here to get any homicidal ideas from the program, it switched to a commercial about a group of teenagers raving over a new salsa, and an idea suddenly started to come together in my mind. Sukie and I usually just snacked on whatever we could scavenge from the kitchen, but it might be fun to have some *real* food for a change.

Gradually, the idea grew and took shape. At work tonight, I'd ask Lupe to make a few of his specialties to go, and I'd even ask Doug if he'd mix us up a batch of margaritas—the risk-free variety, of course. The more I thought about it, the more excited I got. Sukie loved Mexican food, and I was sure she'd be thrilled when she saw the spread I'd brought home for us.

I scrambled to find the big jug Thermos we sometimes used for camping trips, figuring it would be perfect to keep the margaritas cold on the ride home. I hoped the whole dinner wouldn't cost too much; Mom had left me twenty dollars for emergencies, but if it cost more than that I'd have to have Frank put it on my tab until the next time I got paid. I'd deposited my last paycheck in my car savings account at the bank.

After I'd located the Thermos, I got changed for work, humming mariachi tunes to myself. The sleepover with Sukie was going to be even more fun than I'd expected, and

I knew she'd think so, too. It would be the most fun she'd had in a long time, I told myself, and it would remind her of what a great friend I was. I quickly cut off the next thought before it could finish forming, but I knew what the gist of it had been: *Even better,* I hoped, *than her new cheerleader friends.*

sixteen

"*Sí*, I can make some food for you, *señorita*," Lupe said when I'd asked him. His brown eyes twinkled as he flashed his white smile, which looked even whiter against his heat-flushed skin. "Something special happening tonight?" Lupe glanced towards HWSNBN, who was busy scraping out a roaster in which Julio had accidentally burned the chicken for the *pollo a las brasas*.

"No, not really," I replied quickly. "My best friend's spending the night and I thought it would be fun to have some really good food for a change." At that, Lupe beamed and I knew that I'd said the right thing. I told him what time I thought I'd be finished with work, and reminded him to write up a ticket for the food as if I were a regular customer.

Doug, too, seemed pleased to help out.

"Just make us however many will fit in the jug," I told him. "And I'll pay for them, of course. My parents left me some money. They're just away overnight. That's why my friend is sleeping over."

"Ah," Doug said. "I get it. Ladies' night."

"Exactly."

Doug looked thoughtful. "And did you want the regular margaritas, or something special?" He winked.

Confused, I winked back. "Uh … strawberry would be fine," I told him. "That last one you made for me was *magnifico*."

"Gotcha. Don't worry about a thing." Doug took the jug from me. "I'll have this ready when you leave tonight."

I told him he was the best and went back to my post. It was a busy dinner rush, and since I was only there for a short time I didn't even take a break. HWSNBN waved to me a couple times when he came out to help Donna and Cherilyn keep up with clearing tables, but before I knew it, Frank was telling me I could take off.

I'd been a little worried about the cost of the food, so I was surprised and relieved when Lupe refused to let me pay for it. "You and your friend just enjoy it," he said, flapping his hand at me when I asked for the bill. "It's my treat. I already cleared it with Frank."

I protested, but he wouldn't change his mind, so I accepted the fragrant bag of food he'd thoughtfully packed inside one of our TO GO bags, with *Adobe Oven* printed in big, adobe-colored letters across the outside.

Doug gave me the same story. "It's on me," he said, and wouldn't take no for an answer. He handed me the jug, which he'd wiped clean of any stickiness. "Just don't drink it too fast," he teased, tapping his finger against his temple. I was about to tell him that I was no stranger to brain freeze when I felt someone come up behind me.

It was HWSNBN, looking embarrassed. "Lupe told

me you've got too much to carry on your bicycle. He said I can take a few minutes off and run you home, if you want." His face was red, and I knew the ride had probably been Lupe's idea and not his. I was sure he didn't want to be reminded of the last time he gave me a ride home.

I shook my head. "That's okay. Really, I can handle it." Since we had somehow worked our way past the uncomfortable past without discussing it, the best thing to do was to avoid any chance of further awkwardness.

HWSNBN eyed my load, looking doubtful. "Are you sure?" He mimicked what I'd probably look like careening down the street, juggling my load of food.

"Don't worry about it," I said, laughing. "But thanks anyway."

In the end, it turned out that balancing a sloshing jug of strawberry margaritas and an enormous, steaming bagful of Lupe's *tamales* while riding home on Michael's bike *was* more difficult than I'd anticipated. By the time I'd made it halfway home, my arms and back were aching and I wished I'd taken HWSNBN up on his offer. There was no turning back at that point, however, so I figured out how to hang onto both the jug and the food with one arm, and steer the bike with the other. Nevertheless, it hadn't been an easy ride and I was glad when I coasted into the driveway.

"Hey, Scoob!" I yelled as I came in the back door. He could smell the food and was jumping crazily around, hoping some of it was for him. Fortunately, I managed to fend him off and made it over to the counter, where I set everything down and shook the exhaustion out of my arms.

In spite of everything, I arrived home earlier than

expected. Sukie wasn't due to arrive for another forty-five minutes or so; we'd probably have to reheat the food once she got here. I went to put the jug of margaritas in the refrigerator, then changed my mind. After the hellishly hot ride home, I was sweaty and parched. A glass of strawberry sweetness sounded like pure heaven.

It occurred to me that I'd seen some of Mom and Dad's margarita glasses hiding on the top shelf of one of the cupboards, so I climbed up and retrieved two of them. They were a little dusty, but with a quick wipe of the dish-cloth they were ready to go. I poured myself a glassful of margarita, then stored the Thermos in the refrigerator. One swallow and ... *ahhh*; it was just what I needed.

The first taste struck me as a bit more sour than usual, and I wished that I had some special crystallized sugar to put around the rim of the glass, like Doug always used. Still, it was delicious and refreshing, and I took a few more swallows before being hit with the early stirrings of brain freeze. *Slow down, sister,* I reminded myself.

I hummed a mambo to myself as I got out Mom's most colorful table decorations for our Mexican fiesta. When I was finished, the kitchen definitely looked festive. I realized that I'd somehow finished my margarita; I didn't want to fill up before we ate, but I figured that one more wouldn't hurt, so I refilled my glass from the jug in the refrigerator.

It seemed like only a moment later that the second one was gone and I was pouring a third; I couldn't believe how good they were! Doug had filled the Thermos all the way to the top; there would still be plenty when Sukie arrived. "La cucaracha, la cucaracha!" I sang to Scooby, picking him up and dancing around the kitchen. I was feeling a little giddy, so excited to have an entire night to spend hanging out with Sukie. "Just like old times," I confided to Scooby, who regarded me quizzically from his perch in my arms.

I glanced at the clock again, frowning. She must be running late, I thought, fending off the twinge of annoyance that threatened to creep in. Just then the doorbell rang, however. "Aunt Sukie's here!" I told Scooby, whirling us both in a circle before setting him back on the floor. I attempted to head towards the front room, but found that everything had suddenly gone terribly out of kilter. I'd stopped spinning, but the room kept right on going. My path to the front door veered over towards the couch. I fell onto it, laughing at the strangeness of it all.

When the doorbell rang again, I managed to partially recover and struggle to my feet. "I'm *coming!*" I yelled across the living room. *"Keep your pom-poms on!"* For some reason, it was as difficult to get the words to come out in the right order as it was to make it the rest of the way across the room. By the time I finally pulled the front door open, I realized that something was seriously wrong with this picture. "Guess what…I think thoshe marbaritas were…" I slurred, then trailed off.

It wasn't Sukie standing on my front step, ready to apologize for her lateness. Instead, Bonnie's aging gray carcass leaned wearily against the curb, and the person outside my front door—the person staring at me with his mouth hanging open, and his camel-lashed hazel eyes wide—was HWSNBN.

The Chugach Mountains | Alaska's Chugach State Park.

July 16th

Darling Lucy,

Rose and Arlene had to talk me into taking this Alaskan cruise, but I'm certainly glad they did! Alaska is the last true frontier, and it's thrilling to see it with my own eyes. Yesterday we celebrated Arlene's birthday, and we teased her about who was older, Arlene or the glaciers. She laughed, but I don't think she appreciated it!

Remember this: I love you!

Nana Lucy
(definitely younger than a glacier!)

seventeen

"Uh, the place was slow, so Lupe let me leave early," HWS-NBN explained, holding my arm to steady me on my way back across the living room. Things were spinning dangerously now, and I'd allowed him to guide me away from the door and towards the couch. "He was still worried that you'd have an accident carrying all that food home on your bike, so he asked me to stop by and make sure you'd made it home."

"I got here *jusht fine*," I told him, sinking onto the couch. The words came out louder than I'd intended. I lowered my voice to a confidential whisper. *"But I don't think Doug made the right kind of margaritas ... "* I smiled at him goofily, stretching my eyes wide like his, and after a moment he gave up and laughed.

"I think you may be right," he agreed. "Um, maybe you should eat something."

"Yesh! There's food in the kitchen!" I remembered suddenly. "Leth go have shome!" I jumped to my feet with the intention of leading the way, but the ground shifted under me and I stumbled forward, right into HWSNBN who was still standing there, looking worried.

"Whoa!" he said, bracing himself to catch me. Scooby, who had been lying on the floor nearby, barked in alarm, then ran out of the room to avoid being crushed by falling bodies.

HWSNBN's arms around me felt strong and I leaned my head against his chest, suddenly too wobbly to hold myself up. This close to him, I could smell his guy-scent: a combination of Dial soap, clean sweat, and Mexican food. "Mmm," I murmured, snuggling my face into the cozy spot under his chin. "You smell nice."

I felt him tense slightly, then relax, and a moment later his lips moved against my hair. "So do you," he whispered. "Um, Lucy, maybe this isn't a great time, but..."

He trailed off, and after a moment I lifted my head from its comfy place on his chest to see why.

"Well!" came a familiar voice from behind me. "Isn't this a surprise?"

When I turned, the sight that greeted me cut through my margarita haze like a bucket of cold water.

Sukie was standing in the doorway to the kitchen, her pale face a study in disbelief, confusion, and anger. "What in the hell is this, Lucy?" she demanded. She started to add something else, but then her mouth snapped shut and she took a step backwards, nearly stumbling over Scooby, who was snuffling around her legs.

It started becoming clear to me: how she'd come in through the back door without knocking, like she always did, and how she'd come across a surprising scene that, for the moment, I found too complicated to explain.

I backed unsteadily away from HWSNBN, wishing that I could shut out sight of Sukie's stricken, furious face. I knew that if I closed my eyes, though, I'd probably fall over. "Sukie," I said, although I had no idea what was going to come out of my mouth beyond that. "There's nothing... it's not what you... Doug made us the wrong... "

By the time I got that far, she was gone. The back door slammed behind her, and a few seconds later we heard Olive pealing out of the driveway.

I felt for the couch and lowered myself back down onto it miserably. No matter how many margaritas I'd had, I knew that as terrible as I thought things were now, they were going to seem *much* worse once my head cleared.

HWSNBN sank down beside me. "I told you that chick hates me," he said, mystified. "Did you see her face when she saw me here with you?"

I pressed my fingers to my temples, trying to think clearly. "Listen," I told him, forming my words carefully. "It's too much for me to explain right now. All I can say is that for her to walk in and see us together like that... well, I'm not sure which one of us she's going to hate more after this."

"Shheesh," he said. "Maybe I don't *want* to know more."

I sighed, then took a deeper breath. Suddenly, the room seemed too small, and I didn't feel like I was getting enough air. A clammy film of sweat broke out over my entire body. "Uh, I think maybe I should lie down... " I said.

Right before I threw up Doug's totally risky strawberry margaritas, all over HWSNBN.

eighteen

"Man, that stuff is really *red*," HWSNBN said, handing me his strawberry-stained shirt. I'd found him one of Michael's T-shirts to put on while I put his in the washing machine. He was too polite to mention the terrible sweet-sick smell hanging in the air.

"I'm sorry," I moaned for the zillionth time when I returned to the kitchen after getting the washing machine started. I sank into a chair and rested my woozy head on the table. "I'm really, *really* sorry; I feel like a complete, disgusting moron."

I wanted nothing more than to crawl down the hall to my bed, but I could hardly send HWSNBN out without his shirt. "You know what?" I suggested. "Why don't you just wear that shirt tonight and I'll bring yours to you at work."

He considered. I could only imagine that he wanted to leave as badly as I wanted him to. "Maybe I should stay a little longer," he finally said. "I don't really think you should be left alone when you're still so ... in this condition."

I couldn't hold it together any longer. *"Please* go," I

begged, tears springing to my eyes. "I just need to go to bed." Second on the agenda was burying my head under my pillow and having a good cry over how humiliated I felt.

I lifted my sorry head to look at him and was both surprised and relieved to see that the expression on his face was more sympathetic than disgusted.

"How about this," he proposed. "We'll put you to bed and I'll just hang out and watch TV for a little while. Once I'm sure you're asleep for the night, I'll lock up and take off."

I was too tired and miserable to argue. "Fine." I pushed my chair back from the table. I was still a little woozy, but it seemed for a moment as if things might be getting better. Making my way down the hallway to my bedroom, I only careened towards the wall twice, and both times I managed to catch myself.

When I got to my room it was easy to collapse on the bed, since I hadn't bothered to make it after my extended nap earlier that day. I'd thought lying down would feel better, but the minute I closed my eyes the room began spinning wildly, and it wasn't long before I was on my feet, stumbling down the hall towards the bathroom. I was sick again—the cloyingly sweet smell of strawberries mixed with the sour smell of stomach acid made my insides lurch and twist long after there was anything left to come up.

I lifted my head to see HWSNBN standing in the bathroom doorway. "Ugh, I want to die," I moaned. "For more reasons than you can imagine."

He took the hand towel from its rack next to the bathroom sink and dampened it under the tap. "Here," he said, dabbing my face gently with it. "Listen, don't worry about it. It can happen to anyone."

The cool, damp cloth felt good against my skin. Plus, I couldn't help but appreciate how totally sweet he was being. "Thanks," I murmured, feeling more humbled than I'd ever felt in my entire life. "It's just ... I'm not really a drinker. As you can probably tell." The truth was, I wasn't a drinker *at all*. I'd tasted beer before, but I didn't like the taste, and it had never occurred to me to drink anything harder.

"Well, like I said, don't worry about it," HWSNBN replied.

We stood there for a moment, regarding my ghastly reflection in the bathroom mirror. "This wasn't exactly the kind of party I'd had in mind for tonight," I said tiredly.

"Yeah, and when I said I wanted to get together some-time, this wasn't exactly what I had in mind, either," he responded cheerfully. "I was thinking more along the lines of miniature golf, or maybe a movie."

I returned his smile weakly, looking down at my damp, wrinkled clothes. In the mirror, I could see my greenish complexion and wild, sweat-dampened hair. "No kidding? I thought this was what you meant."

"Well, now you'll know for next time." He studied me. "And look at it this way: there's no place to go from here but up."

After a minute, I nodded. "Yes," I whispered faintly. "Okay. Next time."

HWSNBN followed me back down the hallway to my bedroom, then held back the covers as I crawled shakily into bed. I still felt a little queasy, but the spinning of the room seemed slightly less dizzying, and I was weary to my toes. I'd never been tucked into bed by anyone but my parents; it felt strange, but I was too exhausted to be self-conscious about it.

"Looks like you'll probably live," he assessed, "so maybe I'll take off. Unless you want me to stay."

"No ... I'll be fine," I muttered, my eyes closed.

"All right, then ... sleep tight." There was a smile in his voice. A moment later, I felt his lips pressing briefly against my still-clammy forehead. "I'll talk to you later."

"Mm-hmm," I murmured drowsily. I managed to lift my eyelids enough to watch him head out of my room, and a minute later I heard him locking the front door behind him.

As I drifted off, complicated thoughts floated through my brain, but I didn't even try to focus on them. I knew there was lots to sort through, but I'd do it in the morning.

The last thing I heard was Bonnie's low rumble as Jace Turner—formerly known as He Who Shall Not Be Named—pulled away from the curb.

Then I fell into a deep, troubled sleep.

The Burren, County Clare

September 2nd

Hello there, Lassie!

I'd planned to kiss the Blarney Stone when I got to Ireland, but it endows one with "the gift of gab," and I've already got enough of that! Also, you have to do a backbend to reach it, and I stopped doing those when I turned 70.

Remember this: I love you, and Erin go bragh!

Nana Lucy O'Kellogg

LOND

PICCADILLY CIRCUS

Dear Lucy,
Greetings
land of ever
cheese! Sim
the Kirkand
where they
gorgeous
In front of
we were a
countrysqu
esque; it's
Van Gogh
Rimisa
Na

nineteen

"*Mother of God*," I groaned, squinting against the morning rays that were streaming in through my bedroom window. "Does the sun really need to be that bright?" I tried to sit up and immediately fell back on my pillow again with a moan. My head felt as if it had been bisected by a sheet of bright, shiny steel; any movement summoned a blinding flash of metallic-edged pain. My tongue had grown a pasty fur, and the taste in my mouth was a mixture of rotten strawberries, stomach acid, and sludge scraped from the bottom of the garbage disposal. Combining the events of the previous night with the way I felt this morning made it truly impossible for me to understand the allure drinking had for anyone.

An hour later I'd finally managed to climb gingerly out of bed and make my way down the hall to the kitchen for a glass of orange juice. "Crap," I said when I saw the plates of cold *tamales* and beans still sitting on the counter where I'd left them. Unlike cold pizza, Mexican food isn't even remotely appetizing the day after, and *this* morning, it was actually nauseating.

After I let a prancing Scooby outside, I took a hot shower, which went a long way towards making me feel human again. Then I cleaned up the kitchen and dumped the rest of the jug full of margaritas down the sink. I was surprised to see how little was actually left, and I realized that I'd probably drunk a lot more than I'd thought. How many regular-sized margaritas were in a container that large? Six? Eight? If they had been alcohol free, as I'd expected, Sukie would be sitting at the breakfast table with me right now.

No, she wouldn't, I reminded myself. She'd have already gone to cheerleading practice. So far this morning I'd managed to avoid the thought of Sukie, but now that I'd let it in I was forced to remember what had happened. At the recollection of what she'd seen—or what she thought she'd seen—I groaned. There was so much to explain, starting with why I hadn't been honest with my best friend from the first day I found out Jace Turner was working at the AO. The only thing to do was to track her down and start apologizing.

I wandered around the house for another half hour, waiting until I figured Sukie would be home from cheerleading practice. There was no point calling first; I doubted she'd answer if the caller ID showed it was me.

"See ya later," I told Scooby when I couldn't put it off any longer. "Wish me luck." Scooby thumped his tail on the kitchen floor a couple of times in canine sympathy.

"Thanks," I said. "I'll need it."

As I rode Michael's bike over to Sukie's house, the fresh air made my head feel almost normal. I inhaled deeply, trying to calm myself for the confrontation that lay ahead. By the time I rounded the corner to her street and saw Olive parked in her usual place in front of the Hollisters' house, I was actually feeling pretty optimistic. Maybe Sukie would have had enough time to think things through, too, and realize that the whole thing must have been a huge misunderstanding. I even told myself that it might actually turn out to be easy to make things okay again.

The minute Sukie opened the door of the house and I saw her face, however, I knew it wasn't going to be as simple as I'd hoped.

"Hey-y-y..." I trailed off.

Sukie stood in the doorway in her cheerleading practice shorts, staring at me, and made no attempt to respond. Behind her I could see Fiona and several of the other varsity cheerleaders sitting around the kitchen table, where Sukie's mom was pouring them glasses of lemonade from the Hollisters' big pitcher. It must be Sukie's turn to bring everyone home for lunch, I realized.

"Sukie, can I talk to you for a minute? Alone?" I asked her in a low voice. I didn't care to have the entire cheer team informed about the situation, if she hadn't already told them about it.

Sukie didn't respond right away, but after a moment she stepped outside and closed the door behind her.

"Look," I began immediately. "I know that you didn't expect to see Jace Turner at my house last night..." At the sound of his name, Sukie's face grew stony, and I faltered for an instant. "It-It wasn't something I expected either. He just stopped by and ... well, I guess I should have told you earlier: Jace works at the AO too. And I know you probably don't want to hear this, Sukie, but I've gotten to know him a little bit, and he's not such a bad guy. It's just such a coincidence that ..."

"Frankly," Sukie interrupted, her face growing red with anger. "I think it's *no* big coincidence that he's the one person in the world who you knew hurt me the most, and you make sure that he's the one you happen to be making out with ... when you knew I was coming over any second."

"Making out with?" I gaped at her. I might have been intoxicated, but I knew I hadn't been making out with Jace when Sukie showed up.

"It's pretty obvious, don't you think?" Sukie said, leaning towards me in a manner that would have seemed threatening if it wasn't Sukie.

Still, having her angry red face so near made me uncomfortable, and I took a step back, nearly falling off the steps into the shrubbery. "It's obvious?" I repeated blankly.

Sukie nodded. *"Obviously* you resent the fact that I made the cheer team when you didn't, and you wanted to hurt me. You're so jealous you can't stand it, and hooking up with *He Who* ... with Jace Turner was the best way you could think of to get back at me."

My mouth had fallen open as she spoke; there was no way that she could think that I'd set the whole thing up for some kind of twisted revenge. How pathetic and devious did she think I was?

I shook my head in denial, but now I was getting angry too. "First of all, I didn't *hook up* with anybody. And secondly, I can't believe you think I'd be so stupid and jealous as to try and hurt you because I was disappointed that I didn't make cheerleading. I *was* disappointed that I didn't make it; I thought you were disappointed that I didn't make it too! And sure, I do feel a little jealous sometimes. But Sukie, we've been friends since the fourth grade. You know me better than to think I'd do something like that."

She regarded me neutrally, then snorted. "Do I?" she asked.

"Yes." I struggled to calm myself when what I wanted to do was reach out and shake her. "Of course you do."

Sukie's eyes slid away from mine and I experienced a moment of hope that I'd achieved a breakthrough, but then she glanced back towards the front door. "Listen, I've got to go now." She finally brought her eyes back to mine, to make her point. "I have *friends* waiting for me."

"Wait," I pleaded, grabbing for her arm as she turned. I felt like if I just kept explaining, eventually she'd have to hear me.

"Let *GO* of me," she snapped, ripping her arm from my grasp. I wasn't expecting that, and the sudden movement pulled me forward and threw me off balance. In order to avoid falling on Sukie, I threw my body to the right and ended up toppling off the steps and landing gracelessly in the shrubbery below. I heard branches splitting and felt the sharp jab of a twig shoot up into my armpit. *Note to self: Thank Mr. Hollister for not planting his rosebushes next to the front steps.*

"What the *hell*, Sukie?" I roared, unnerved to suddenly find myself lying in the bristly hedge. "What's next? Do you want to fight me in the street?"

A look of uncertainty flashed across Sukie's face as she regarded me lying prone in the Hollisters' hedge. She actually began to lean forward, her hand outstretched, to help me climb out of the bushes. But unfortunately, I was too angry and I kept talking. "You know what?" I spat, "You really *are* a bitch sometimes."

Sukie pulled back as if her hand had been burned. I don't know which of us was more surprised by what I'd said. It didn't matter, I guess. My former best friend spun on her heel and went inside, letting the door slam closed behind her and leaving me lying there in the shrubs.

twenty

Now I was both frustrated with myself and furious that Sukie had been unwilling to try and understand, or at least hear me out. And if I'd caught the meaning of her last remark, she was drawing a strong distinction between her "friends" and *my* standing. Part of my brain was outraged that Sukie would throw away our friendship so easily (and literally), while the other part acknowledged a niggling feeling of guilt that I'd been partly responsible for getting us to this point by not being honest with her. *You made your bed, and now you've actually landed in it.*

I extricated myself gingerly from the Hollisters' landscaping, not looking back at the house where Sukie was. Remounting Michael's bike, I felt hot and itchy, like I'd just wrestled a porcupine; whatever variety the Hollisters' shrubbery was, I hoped I wasn't allergic to it. Or maybe I deserved to be allergic to it. I didn't know anymore.

As I pedaled numbly home, I replayed the conversation with Sukie over and over again, trying to see where I could have said something that might have made a difference in the outcome. In the end, I couldn't think of any other way to approach things except head-on, as I had. Sukie was stubborn, that much I knew, and I'd seen how long she could hold a grudge. With a sigh, I pictured Sukie telling her cheerleader friends that I would henceforth be referred to only as "She Who Shall Not Be Named."

I didn't feel like going home yet, so I rode Michael's bike down Snob Hill and through the older area of town where Mom grew up, letting the wind chase the final cobwebs out of my head. I tried to picture a younger, smaller version of Mom, walking along the sidewalk as a little girl on her way to school at Williston Elementary. I wondered whether she hoped someday she'd have a house on Chess Drive with her husband and four kids. And her mother-in-law, I added. And Alzheimer's disease.

By early afternoon, I realized my legs were getting tired of pedaling, so I rode back to my neighborhood and stopped in Spring Lake Park. I lay on my back in the soft grass, watching the clouds drift overhead. It was something Sukie and I had done together many times, and it felt lonely to do it by myself. "Oh look, that one looks just like a cow," I said experimentally, then looked around quickly to see if anyone had heard me. Two boys who looked to be around eight were playing catch with a football and not paying any attention to me at all. A young mother was watching her toddler playing in the sandbox, but was too far away to hear me. I sighed, feeling more alone than I'd ever felt in my life.

My rumbling stomach finally reminded me I hadn't had anything to eat yet, so I got back on my bicycle and rode the rest of the way home. As I approached, I was surprised to see our Suburban already parked in the driveway. The sight made me glad I'd cleaned up the mess in the kitchen before I left for Sukie's.

When I pulled up, Mom was standing in the garage with Rachel. The last thing I wanted was to have to pretend to be bright and cheery, but they'd already spotted me, so there was no turning back now.

"Hey sweetie, were you over at Sukie's?" Mom called. She has an uncanny ability to know what I've been up to, but I hoped her intuition didn't span beyond the last hour or so. "How was the sleepover?"

"Uh, yeah, it was okay," I said, dancing past the truth. "Um, it was fun." I didn't want to answer any more questions about Sukie, so I changed the subject. "How was the trip?"

"Oh, pretty draining," Mom sighed. "Nana's testing this morning didn't take as long as expected, so we headed home right afterwards." She glanced at her watch. "We made good time, in fact."

I reached past her and grabbed the suitcase she was reaching for. "How did the appointment go?"

"Well, all right," Mom replied. "Clearly they do these sorts of evaluations a lot; both Dr. Thompson and her technician, Tonja, made Nana feel as comfortable as possible. It was pretty stressful for Nana, but she held it together."

She was silent for a moment, watching Rachel, who had gone out to perform handstands on the lawn. "Feels good to get out of the car, right, sweetie?" she called.

"Uh-huh," Rachel replied, upside down.

"Anyway," Mom said, turning back to me, "the results were pretty much what we'd been afraid of. Dr. Thompson thinks Nana Lucy is definitely in the early stages of Alzheimer's. She said there are medications to slow it down, but not to stop it."

"So Nana's going to keep getting more and more confused?"

Mom nodded. "It's hard to predict how quickly it will happen," she said, "but yes, she'll continue to get worse. Dr. Thompson also felt it was best that Nana not return to living independently. She didn't think it would be safe, and I guess I agree with that after what we've seen lately. Aunt Carol met us in Minot and heard the results, so she'll swing by Minneapolis on her way home to pack up Nana's things and get the apartment ready to sell. It'll sell quickly, I hope."

Mom saw my face and stopped talking. As she reached out and pulled me close, I felt hot tears filling my eyes. I rested my head against her shoulder and let them come. "It will be okay," she soothed, rubbing my back in her comforting way. "Nana has a lot of people who love her and we'll do everything possible to make sure that the rest of her life is good."

I cried until I couldn't cry anymore, not caring who drove by and saw us standing there. At one point I felt Rachel's arms coming around me too, and that only made me cry harder. I was crying for all of us; for Nana Lucy the most of course, but also for our family, and for me, and for my former friend, Sukie. It didn't seem fair that everything had to change, and that none of those changes would be good ones.

"Come on, sweetie, let's go inside," Mom said when my tears had slowed. "Dad took Nana Lucy in to lie down, and I want you to pull yourself together before she gets up. She's upset enough as it is, and it will only make her feel guilty if she thinks you're hurting over her."

"Okay." I sniffled, and turned towards the house.

"My goodness, the backs of your arms are all broken out," Mom exclaimed. "What happened?"

"Oh ... I was lying in the grass down at the park," I told her, turning my arms over to look. "I guess I must be allergic to something." Sure enough, there were red, streaky welts wherever my arms had come into contact with the Hollisters' shrubbery. And now that I thought about it, they itched.

"Don't scratch," Mom advised as I automatically began doing so. "I'll find you some ointment."

Still carrying the suitcase, I followed Mom into the house, where I would wash my face, apply antihistamine ointment to my scratches, and then act as if nothing else was wrong. Note to self: *You might as well get good at it; it's a skill you're going to need.*

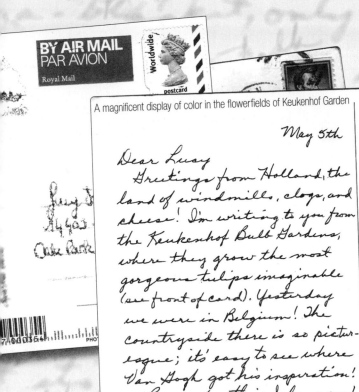

A magnificent display of color in the flowerfields of Keukenhof Garden

May 5th

Dear Lucy
   Greetings from Holland, the
land of windmills, clogs, and
cheese! I'm writing to you from
the Keukenhof Bulb Gardens,
where they grow the most
gorgeous tulips imaginable
(see front of card). Yesterday
we were in Belgium! The
countryside there is so pictur-
esque; it's easy to see where
Van Gogh got his inspiration!
   Remember this: I love you!
      Nana L.

QUEBEC CITY
View from Lévis

GRAPHIC DESIGN ®

twenty-one

"Lucy, could you pass the salsa?" Mom said, and we all laughed when both Nana Lucy and I reached for it at the same time. "I'll get it, Nana," I told her, passing the bowl.

Tired from the trip, my parents had agreed to order dinner out, and wouldn't you know it…everyone had voted for Mexican. I'd declined to go with Dad to pick it up; after last night, I wasn't too keen on seeing anyone from work, especially Jace. I cringed every time I thought of how I'd spewed strawberry all over him, and I'd hidden his laundered-but-still-stained shirt in my dresser drawer under some sweatshirts. Basically, I was stalling, hoping I could avoid the whole thing for a while, or at least until the next day when I was scheduled to work the four-to-ten shift.

"I love the AO's burritos!" Rachel exclaimed around her mouthful of food. Mom shook her head disapprovingly, but smiled. "It is delicious," she agreed. Dad said nothing, but was clearly enjoying his food, too. Although he'd picked up quite a smorgasbord, neither Nana Lucy nor I seemed to have much of an appetite.

"Aren't you hungry, Mother?" Dad motioned to the plateful of food she had barely touched.

Nana Lucy smiled, but her face didn't have its usual light. "I guess not, dear."

"Lucy, we ate at Little Italy last night!" Rachel told me excitedly after she'd swallowed. "It's a new restaurant in Minot where you get to watch while they make your pizza!"

"Cool," I said distractedly, moving the food around my plate to make it look as if I'd eaten some. I didn't trust my stomach to begin with, and the smell of cheese and beans was making me a little queasy.

"If you'll all excuse me, I think I'll go out for some fresh air," Nana Lucy announced, pushing her chair back from the table. As she got up, I saw Mom and Dad trade looks, so I jumped up too.

"How about if I go with you, Nana?" I asked. "I feel like I could use some air too."

Nana Lucy hesitated, then nodded. "Certainly, dear." I suspected that she'd hoped to have some time to herself, but I acted as if I didn't have a clue.

"Let me just grab my flip flops, and I'll be out." I headed to my bedroom, moving quickly. I was worried she might start off without me, but when I got outside, Nana Lucy was standing by the front steps, waiting for me.

We headed down the sidewalk slowly, me looking ahead to anticipate any cracks or uneven places in the pavement that could cause an old lady to stumble. I still wasn't used to this new, slower Nana; in the past, I'd have to hurry to keep up with her.

"So, what did you think of the doctor in Minot?" I asked. Earlier, Mom had said it would be better for Nana Lucy if we talked openly about the evaluation.

"Oh, he was fine," she said. Her eyes were following a robin that was flying from tree to tree, and I wished she'd watch her feet more.

"What did you say...*he* was fine?" I wasn't sure if I'd heard her correctly, and I was sure Mom had said Dr. Thompson was a woman.

"Yes, he was a very nice fellow, and his wife was pleasant, too."

"Nana Lucy, I'm not sure we're talking about the same person," I said slowly. "I'm pretty sure the doctor you saw was a woman."

Nana hesitated. "Oh, well, maybe it was," she finally agreed. "You just never know."

You don't?

"I guess I checked out okay, so that's what's important." Nana Lucy turned to me with a smile.

"Oh...uh-huh," I responded, not sure what else to say. I wondered if Nana Lucy actually didn't remember that the doctor had told her she had Alzheimer's disease, or whether she just didn't want to talk about it right now. If it were me, I'm not sure I'd feel like talking about it either.

We reached the corner and I touched her arm. "Let's go this way," I suggested. "We can walk past the coulee." When the weather turned warm, hordes of ducks take up residence in the coulee that runs along the cornfield that grows a couple blocks west of our house. Last summer, I'd seen a huge snapping turtle hiding in the tall grasses along the edge. I figured Nana Lucy might enjoy seeing the wildlife, and I would too.

We walked to the edge of the coulee. I didn't dare wander down the uneven bank to get a closer look with Nana Lucy along, so we enjoyed the view from the sidewalk.

"I just love summertime," Nana Lucy said suddenly, reaching out to squeeze my hand. "It's my favorite time of year."

I smiled, forgetting everything but how much I loved her. "Mine too." I squeezed back gently. Her fingers felt as fragile as twigs.

"I just remembered this," she said suddenly, stopping. Her eyes grew dreamy and she smiled. "When I was a little girl, my daddy and brothers would go out to work in the fields, under the hot sun. My mother would send me out to the fields with a jug of water for them. Daddy called me his little Molly Pitcher."

"Really?" I hadn't heard this story before.

"Yes." She nodded. "The first time Mama let me go by myself, I wanted to take the water to them as quickly as I could, because I knew how hot and thirsty they would be. I ran across the fields as fast as my little legs would carry me, but by the time I got to them, nearly half the water had sloshed out of the pitcher! After that, I remembered to walk slowly, even though it was hard. I just loved to see their faces when I came walking out of the wheat; they were so excited to see me and my jug of cool water!"

Nana Lucy sighed, lost in happy memories. Her parents

had died before I was born, and her brothers were gone too. She's the last one, I realized suddenly. The only member of her family left. After she was gone, a whole generation would have passed, and life would move forward with the next generation.

In some ways, it already seemed as if Nana Lucy herself was fading away, evaporating before my eyes like a ghost. The thought of her disappearing entirely brought a painful lump to my throat. "Remember this, Nana," I told her earnestly. "I love you." Our "remember this" had taken on a whole new meaning.

Nana smiled at me, her eyes soft. "Why, I love you too, Lucy-bell," she said.

We admired a group of ducklings following their mother down the coulee in an orderly line, and vowed that next time we came this way we'd bring bread crumbs for them. When it finally seemed time for us to continue on our way, I led us down a side street and back around the block towards home. It seemed like everything we saw reminded Nana Lucy of something or other from her past, and she provided an interesting commentary to our trip, pointing out a porch like the one she'd grown up with, and a small boy whose shock of unruly hair reminded her of her younger brother, Richard. Nana seemed surprised and a little disappointed when I led her back up the driveway to our house and announced we were home.

"Oh my," she said. "Is this where you live? What a lovely place."

I bit my lip. We'd been having such a nice time that it came as a shock to think that Nana Lucy might have forgotten where we were headed, or worse, that I was her granddaughter.

"It's our house, remember, Nana?" I said gently, looking in her eyes. They were still a clear, pale blue, the color that my grandfather used to call "cornflower." "Remember? I'm Lucy, your granddaughter. And your son Bruce lives here, and your daughter-in-law, Margo..."

I continued naming family members until suddenly the fog seemed to clear and the puzzled look disappeared from her face. *"Lucy!"* she said, "Why, of course you're my granddaughter. I don't know why, but that just didn't seem right for a minute."

She reached out with both hands and put them on either side of my face, then gave me a quick kiss on the tip of my nose. "My heavens, but it's warm out here. Shall we go inside and see if your mother has any lemonade in the refrigerator?"

"Sounds perfect," I replied, slipping an arm protectively through hers as we headed towards the house. "Let's find out."

twenty-two

The next morning I thought about calling in sick, but I knew I couldn't put off facing Jace indefinitely. "Hey, stranger!" Cherilyn called when she saw me coming through the door. "Long time, no see!"

"Yeah," I smiled sheepishly. "It's been a couple days." Usually I'd stick my head around the corner and say hello to Doug and anyone else who might be within shouting distance, but today I stuck close to the hostess station. But once the lunch crowd began arriving, there was nothing I could do to avoid the main dining room. I'd just seated a table and was making a beeline back to the front when I heard Doug calling to me from behind the bar.

"Psst, Lucy," he hissed, "come here for a second."

Reluctantly, I veered off track and headed over to the bar. "Listen," he said when I got close, "your boyfriend gave me hell for those margaritas. I thought we were on the same page about the whole thing, but I guess we got our wires crossed."

Two things about what Doug said made me pause

before I responded: the fact that he'd called Jace my boyfriend, for one, and the idea that Jace had "given Doug hell" for putting me in a bad situation, for another.

"Yeah, you can say that again," I responded finally. "What gave you the idea I wanted alcohol in them?" I wondered how many other people knew.

"You told me that your parents weren't home, and I thought it was kind of your way of saying, well, you know. Why else did you think I told you to drink 'em slow?" Doug glanced around, looking guilty, and it occurred to me that he could get in a lot of trouble if Frank or anyone else found out. I relaxed, realizing it was unlikely that anyone else at the AO knew.

"I guess I thought you meant something else," I admitted. "Well ... it was quite a night."

He smiled. "According to your boyfriend, that's an understatement."

"He's not my boyfriend," I clarified.

"So, listen," Doug continued. "I'll be out on the street if Frank hears about this, so I'd appreciate it if you didn't say anything. Kind of our little secret, okay?"

"Fine by me," I agreed, relieved it wasn't going to be a topic of gossip around the restaurant. "But do *me* a favor. The next time you decide to make my margaritas full strength, let me know, okay?"

"Deal." Doug nodded over my shoulder and I turned to see Frank leading a group of women to a booth near the window, looking pointedly at me as he went.

"I'd better go." I hurried back to the front, where I belonged.

The lunch rush was steady but not overtaxing, so everyone was still in fairly good spirits by the time it tapered off. "Whew, I'm glad that's over with," Donna breathed, resting her tray on the countertop beside the till. A minute later, Verona came around the corner looking for her. "How are you doing in tips, D? That big table left me a lousy five bucks."

"I'm not doing too badly today," Donna shrugged. "Last night sucked though. Say, Miss Lucy," she said, turning to me, "I heard loverboy stopped by your place the other night."

"You did?" I wondered whether I'd been wrong about people knowing what had gone on.

"Yeah, Lupe said he asked him to stop by and check that you'd made it home all right. He said the guy jumped at the chance; he couldn't get out of here fast enough. Even left a pile of dirty dishes that Julio had to wash … boy, was he mad!"

"Huh." I smiled in spite of myself. "Well, I guess I'll take my break now."

Donna narrowed her eyes. "Oh *no,* you don't," she grinned, waggling her finger at me. "You're not going anywhere until you cough up some juicy details. Did he show up at your place? And by the way, weren't you supposed to be having a slumber party?"

I studied my fingernails, pretended to be finding them very interesting, but the waitresses weren't buying it. "Come on," Verona said. "Give us the dirt. Are you two finally *enamorado?*"

I looked up suddenly, as if I'd just heard my name

being called. "I think Frank needs me for something..." I made as if to head towards the back.

Donna blocked me with her tray. "Frank went downstairs to the office a half hour ago," she said. "As we all know. Now if you don't tell us what happened, we're going to go right to the source himself. I'm sure he'll talk if we hold his head under the dishwater for a while..."

"Okay!" I yelped, laughing. "I'll tell you, but it's not nearly as exciting as you're hoping."

"Listen, honey, our lives are pretty dull," Verona reminded me, gesturing to the emptying restaurant. "We'll take whatever you've got."

"Speak for yourself," Donna told her.

Still, they both leaned in to hear what I was going to say. "Well," I began, wondering how to say enough to satisfy them without revealing the actual horror of Tuesday night. "He stopped over right before my friend got there..."

Donna's smile grew in anticipation. "So the two of you were alone?"

"Well, just for a few minutes. And then... he saw that I was okay, so he left." It was a greatly abridged version, but none of it was an out-and-out lie.

Verona looked nonplussed. "That was it?" she said. "No flirting? No kissing?"

"Sorry," I told her apologetically. "But it *was* really sweet of him to stop by." I tried not to think about Jace's freshly washed T-shirt in my purse under the counter. Some of the red stain had washed out, but not all of it; there was still a Rorschach blot of pink across the front. I wouldn't have bothered to bring it back at all, except I figured he could maybe use it to wash Bonnie. Plus, it would have been awkward for me to ask for Michael's T-shirt back without returning his, and though I figured there was little chance my brother would miss it, I didn't want to take any chances.

"Humph," Donna said, obviously disappointed. "So that's it, huh? Well, it's a waste. He's a cutie pie."

"Yep, you'd better watch out or someone else will snap him up!" Verona gestured towards Donna, who waggled her eyebrows in comical agreement.

I smiled, thinking of the soft kiss Jace had left on my forehead. *"Que sera, sera*, I guess."

Just then, Jace himself came around the corner, and Verona and Donna scattered like buckshot, giggling. "Hey," he said, smiling when he saw me. "How's it going?"

The sight of him unexpectedly filled my stomach with flittering butterflies. "A lot better than the last time you saw me," I said sheepishly, feeling my face grow warm.

He grinned. "Yeah, you look a little better."

I reached under the counter and pulled his T-shirt out of my purse. "Here." I figured no further explanation was necessary. "It's as clean as I could get it, anyway."

Jace tucked it under his arm without looking at it. "I've got your brother's out in my car," he said in a low voice.

"Okay." For some reason, I was having trouble looking at him.

"Hey listen," Jace said. "I came up here to ask you if you work tomorrow night."

"Yep, but just until five. Why?"

"Well, I've got the night off, and I was wondering if you'd maybe like to, you know … do something after you get done with work. Hang out or something." He said it casually, but I could tell by the tension in his jaw that he was nervous about asking.

"Uh …" I stalled, thinking. I thought about Sukie telling me I was trying to hurt her because I was jealous and spiteful. I thought how ridiculous I must have looked, lying in the Hollisters' shrubbery, and how she went inside without even helping me get up.

I swallowed and smiled at Jace, who visibly relaxed. "You know what? I would love that. Why don't you pick me up around seven?"

We beamed at each other for a split second, during which I noticed that his teeth were perfect and I liked the way his hair kind of hung over one eye. "All right then," he said, rubbing his hands together awkwardly. "I guess I'd better get back to work. So … seven then? We could get some dinner."

"Perfect," I agreed. "You know where I live, I guess."

"I guess I do," he replied, smiling. "So, okay, *great*." He backed out of sight around the corner. I didn't have to check with Donna and Verona; their beaming faces across the dining room told me that we were all in agreement.

Note to self: Looks like you've made your choice, Lucy Kellogg. Too bad you had to.

Worldwide
postcard

Neuschwanstein in Abend.

LOND

PICCADILLY CIRCUS

August 26th

Guten Tag, Fraulein Lucy,
   I'm writing this from Bavaria,
and the castle on the front is
Neuschwanstein, home of King
Ludwig (aka "Mad King Ludwig").
One room is entirely devoted to
the 36 women he loved; I'm
glad Grandpa Sam was a one-
woman man!
   Remember this: I love you!
      Nana Lucy
   (aka "Mad Nana Lucy")

Dear Lucy,
   Greetings
Land of won
cheese! I'm
the Trukha
where the
gorgeous
In front of
we were
courtyard
esque; it
Van Gogh
Lessons
N

twenty-three

"So what can you tell me about this character?" Dad said when I announced that I had a date. I'd just ridden up on Michael's bike to find him washing the bugs out of the Suburban's grill. Even for a Friday, the restaurant had been busy, and it was nearly six by the time I'd gotten out of there. I knew I'd have to make it through the question-and-answer period quickly if I wanted to have enough time before Jace showed up to rinse away the *eau de taco* I was wearing.

"He's a normal kid, Dad. He goes to my school and he washes dishes at the AO. Completely harmless, I promise."

Dad made a face of mock disapproval. "Well, you know what they say about dishwashers, Lucy."

"I know, I know … most serial killers were once dish-washers."

"Well," Dad continued, "who are his parents? Do Mom and I know them?"

I sighed, a little exasperated. What was this … 1957? "We haven't gotten that far, Dad. You can ask him when he gets here and then we'll both know. Listen, I've got to jump in the shower."

Dad waved me away and went back to scrubbing the Suburban's grill, but I knew what he was thinking. I'd gone out with a couple of boys over the years, but they were group dates. This was my first real date, alone with a boy.

I took my shower, taking care to rinse my hair twice in case there was any greasy food smell still clinging to it. When I came out of the bathroom wrapped in a towel, Nana Lucy and Mom were just coming in from their evening walk.

"So, Dad tells us that you've got a big evening planned," Mom said with a smile. Nana Lucy twinkled at me.

"It's *no big deal*," I told them. "Jace is just a guy I know from work. We'll probably just grab a bite to eat or something."

"This is your first real date, sweetie," Mom gushed. "I'm so excited. Would you be embarrassed if I took a picture?"

"Holy crap, Mom...I will absolutely die if you bring out the camera like my having a date is a once-in-a-lifetime event or something. Promise me that you won't. *Promise me!*"

The little lines around Mom's eyes crinkled in the way they do when she's trying not to laugh. "All right, don't have a coronary. I'm just excited, that's all. Did you call Sukie? What does she think? Is she excited for you?"

I nodded, swallowing hard. "Uh-huh." I forced a smile on my face and hoped my voice didn't sound as strangled as it felt. I didn't even want to think about what

Sukie would have to say if she knew I was going out on a date with Jace Turner. Although maybe by this point, she wouldn't be surprised. "Well, I guess I'd better go finish getting ready."

"Don't hurry," Nana Lucy advised. "A gentleman expects to wait for a lady."

Ugh. There was nothing to say to a comment like that. I just hoped they wouldn't all be hanging around, staring, when Jace arrived. I hurried down the hallway to my bedroom and tried to decide what to wear. Serena had left me a fairly good selection of hand-me-downs, so it usually seemed like I had plenty of clothes to choose from. I finally settled on a denim skirt and a soft yellow top from Abercrombie & Fitch. Mom said she refused to pay forty dollars for a T-shirt, but Serena had left it behind when she'd come home from college at spring break.

I dried my hair and was spritzing on some perfume when I heard the doorbell. *"Lucy!"* Rachel called, her voice sing-songy with significance. "There's someone *here* for you."

I said a silent prayer that my family wouldn't completely humiliate me, threw on a pair of sandals, and hurried down the hall towards the living room.

"Hi..." I stopped in my tracks. Sukie stood there, her face tense but her expression carefully neutral.

"You left some things at my house," she said. "Some books and clothes and stuff. I thought you'd be at work, so I wanted to drop them off. But I guess you're here, so..." She held out a brown paper bag, folded over at the top.

I took it, my mouth as dry as if it, too, was lined with rough brown paper. Rachel, who had settled onto the couch in front of the television, had looked up to watch the scene with interest.

Still, I suddenly had the urge to try one last time. "Sukie," I said desperately, "you've got to let me explain. I know what things looked like and what it *seemed* like, but that's not..."

And *of course*, at that very moment, the worst possible thing happened: there was another knock on the door, and we all turned as if controlled by one puppeteer to see Jace Turner standing on our front steps, looking through the screen door. He raised a hand and waved uncertainly when he saw Sukie. After the drama that had unfolded during his previous visit, I could imagine why the sight of her might make him apprehensive.

Sukie turned slowly to face me again, and now everything about her face was masklike. "That's okay...I was leaving anyway." She backed away from me stiffly.

"Sukie...wait," I said hopelessly, but she spun on her heel and took off out the door, pushing past Jace. He stepped back quickly, out of her way.

"Lucy?" Mom appeared in the kitchen doorway. "What's going on?" I hadn't even heard her come up behind me, and wondered how much she'd seen. On the couch, Rachel's eyes were wide, but she said nothing.

With a confusing mixture of feelings, I pulled myself together and crossed the room to open the door for Jace, who was still standing outside on the front step. "Mom, Rachel," I said as he stepped inside, "this is Jace Turner. Jace, this is my mom and my little sister, Rachel."

Jace shook their hands and I watched as Mom smiled

and greeted him politely, although I could tell by her subtle hesitancy that she was still confused by whatever she'd seen happen between me and Sukie. Rachel had forgotten about everything but Jace, and was staring at him as if he were a movie star. Scooby was snuffling at the leg of Jace's jeans as if he suspected Jace had a rabbit hidden up there somewhere.

"Rachel, run out to the back yard and get your father," Mom told her. "I'm sure these two would like to get going, but I know Dad will want to meet Jace before they leave."

"You have to meet my grandmother, too," I told Jace, who was looking a little overwhelmed by all the attention. "She's out in the kitchen." I led him into the kitchen, where Nana Lucy was sitting at the kitchen table, sipping a glass of root beer and playing solitaire. "Nana," I said, "This is Jace Turner."

"It's lovely to meet you, Mr. Turner," Nana said. She smiled and looked at him appraisingly. "You remind me very much of my husband, Samuel, when I first met him."

Jace colored, but he grinned. "It's nice to meet you too," he replied. "Mrs. ...."

"Her name's Lucy Kellogg, same as mine," I told him proudly. "I'm named after Nana Lucy."

"You two young people have a nice time," Nana Lucy said. "And you take good care of our Lucy," she added, looking directly at Jace.

"Yes, ma'am." He looked at me with a smile that still gave me goose bumps. "I will."

Although I'd thought that Jace meeting Dad would be the worst, I was pleasantly surprised when Dad just shook

Jace's hand and asked him about his car. "She's an '87 Bonneville, Mr. Kellogg," Jace told him. "She's an oldie, but she runs. I'm saving up to buy something newer before I go to college."

I could see that Jace's future plans won points with both my parents *and* Nana Lucy, and I decided we should leave while we were ahead.

"Speaking of Bonnie..." I said, gesturing towards the door. When Jace looked away, I made a face at Rachel, who was lingering in the room so as not to miss anything.

"Bonnie? Are you meeting up with another friend?" Nana asked, but Dad laughed.

"I think she's referring to Jace's car, Mother. I named my first car, too." He looked nostalgic. "She was a Chevy Impala, so I called her Paula." Mom laughed out loud, and Dad looked sheepish.

Once outside, I apologized. "And that was their best behavior," I told Jace.

"No, they're really nice." He grinned. "And don't worry, I'm sure my family will put you through the same drill."

He opened the passenger door for me and I climbed inside, then he ran around and got in the driver's seat. "Shall we get this train on the tracks, then?" he asked, reaching over and surprising my hand with a sudden squeeze.

"Let's do it." I smiled. It was my favorite time of day; the sun was sinking lower in the sky and the clouds were streaked with shades of gold, pink, and lavender. I relaxed, but a sudden vision of Sukie's shocked, wounded face intruded on my happiness. I squeezed my eyes closed, determined to push it away for at least the next couple of hours.

twenty-four

As the early evening sun began to wane, we took a turn down Main Street just to see who was out and about. I kept my eye peeled for Olive, but relaxed once we'd completed the Main Street circuit with no sign of her.

"Are you hungry yet?" Jace asked. "I could use something to eat."

"Yeah, starving." I hadn't eaten before work, and there'd been no time to grab anything once I got home. As if seconding that notion, my stomach rumbled its agreement.

Jace steered Bonnie into the Burger Time lot; I expected him to park, but instead he pulled into the drive-through lane.

"Welcome-to-Burger-Time-Can-I-Take-Your-Order?"

Jace turned to me. "What'll it be?" he asked, smiling.

I leaned around him to see the menu. "A cheeseburger and fries. With extra mustard. And a diet Coke."

Jace repeated my order, then ordered a double bacon cheeseburger, French fries, and a vanilla shake for himself.

I've never understood how boys manage to eat so much food.

The disembodied voice instructed us forward to the pick-up window, where we waited for our order.

"So, you're wanting to eat in the car?" I asked.

Jace smiled. "Actually, I know a great place where we can go to eat. I go there myself sometimes if I need to be alone to think about things."

I wondered what kind of things Jace liked to think about when he was alone. "Really? Where?"

"You'll see."

"All right," I said, feigning doubt. I didn't know if it was the waning golden sunlight or what, but suddenly Jace was so good-looking that I wondered whether I'd even be able to eat at all, no matter where it was he took me.

A moment later, a pimply faced boy slid the pick-up window open and handed us our food. Jace turned to set the bag in Bonnie's back seat, then leaned towards me to set the cardboard beverage caddy on the floor near my feet. When he did, the light, woodsy scent of his cologne wafted up to my nose. *Mmm*, I thought to myself.

He nosed the car out of the parking lot and onto the street. After driving for a few minutes, I realized he was heading for the old downtown area of Williston.

"Where are we going, exactly?" I asked. I couldn't imagine there would be any place around the aging downtown buildings that would be conducive to peaceful thought.

"You'll see," he said, grinning at my impatience. "We're almost there. In fact, close your eyes; it'll be even better if it's a surprise."

I gave him a "this is cheesy" look, but was secretly charmed by the idea of being transported to some surprise destination. Jace Turner was *full* of surprises, I was learning.

Leaning my head back against the seat, I closed my eyes. It was actually pleasant to ride this way, feeling the evening breeze from the open window whispering across my face. We went over a sudden bump and the noises outside the car suddenly became closer and echo-y. I realized we'd driven inside something, but instead of stopping the car, Bonnie made a sharp left turn, then continued to veer left, round and round in an endless, ascending spiral. "Remember, I have a touchy stomach," I warned ominously, laughing. I had a pretty good idea where we were now, but I didn't want to ruin the surprise.

"How could I forget? Hang on, we're almost there." As we circled, the sounds of the city seemed to fall away, until the only sound left was Bonnie's wheels against the pavement.

"Don't open your eyes yet," Jace said as the car finally came to a stop. I heard his door open, and a minute later he was on my side of the car, opening the door for me. He took my hand and helped me out of my seat. "Okay," he said when I was standing up outside the car, feeling a little dizzy. "You can open your eyes now."

I let my lids go up slowly. Even though I knew where we were, I was still surprised by what I saw. "Oh," I said softly.

As I'd suspected, we were standing on top of the old downtown parking ramp, which was entirely vacant other than Bonnie and the two of us. Far below us, I could hear distant traffic noises, as if we were on top of a mountain, far from civilization. "Look up," Jake said, and when I did, I gasped. The sky above seemed bigger than I had ever seen it, its darkening blue punctuated by a scattering of faint stars.

"Isn't it something?" Jake tipped his own head back to admire the view above us. "When I come up here, it feels like the world, like *life*, is so just so ... unlimited. Like anything is possible, if I just open up my mind. It's weird; sometimes it almost makes me feel like ... crying."

I turned and looked at him, a beautiful boy gazing with wonder at a beautiful sky. My heart swelled with something I'd never felt before. "Thank you for bringing me up here," I told him sincerely. "It's a wonderful place. In fact, it makes me happy just to know someplace like this is here."

Jake nodded, as if he understood just what I meant. "I've never told anyone else that I come here," he said. "But something made me want to show it to you."

A very unromantic grumble from my stomach broke the mood, and Jace set about finding an old blanket in Bonnie's trunk to use as a picnic cloth, spreading it on the concrete floor of the ramp. "Even better than a fancy restaurant," I told him, although I hadn't ever really been in a fancy restaurant. It didn't matter; he grinned anyway. I set out our food and drinks on the blanket and we settled in.

When I bit into my cheeseburger under the brightening stars, I thought I'd never tasted anything so delicious. As night continued to fall, more and more stars seemed to appear until there were millions. The streetlights had come on below us, but they couldn't compete with the view above.

Jake leaned back on his elbows and looked across at

me. "So," he said, "your angry little friend; was she really leaving, or was it just because I showed up?"

I'd succeeded in pushing away any thought of Sukie, and now I didn't want it to ruin the wonderful time I was having. Still, it was probably time for Jace to know the truth, and now was as good of a time as any to tell him the whole story. "Actually," I sighed, "at this point I'm not sure she's in the 'friend' category anymore. 'Angry,' however, is accurate."

Jace looked surprised. "You're not even friends anymore? What happened? I thought you said she was your *best* friend."

I sighed. "Yeah, well, apparently our friendship wasn't as indestructible as I wanted to think. She's ready to write me out of her life because ... well, because of you."

Jace's eyebrows lifted in surprise. "Because of me? You're going to have to explain this to me. You said you would, anyway."

"Yeah." I took a deep breath. "Well, do you remember back when we were freshman? You were in my ... our ... first period class?"

He nodded. "Yeah, Hoffman's algebra class."

"Uh-huh. Well, Sukie had a huge crush on you, which probably was pretty obvious."

Jace thought about it. "I don't really remember," he admitted. "I know we studied together that one time, although I was kind of surprised when she wanted to. It seemed like she knew more about the stuff than I did."

"Right. Well, then you were going to get together again to study for some test we were having, but then you sent her those text messages, and well, frankly... you were kind of a jerk in them."

Now he looked confused. "I did? I was? What did I say?"

I thought back, then stared up at the starry sky while I repeated as much as I could remember. "And then you said something like, 'Right back at you, bitch.' I turned to look at him.

Jace was looking at me with an expression of complete surprise and bewilderment on his face. "Oh, don't pretend like you don't remember," I sighed, disappointed that he'd try to pull this.

"Lucy." He was shaking his head slowly. "I don't." When I raised my eyebrows doubtfully, he repeated it. "I *don't*. I swear to you. Are you sure it was me she was texting with?"

"I know it was you," I said. "It was a Saturday morning, and you were bowling. You had a bowling date with..."

"...Sarah," he finished. "I went bowling with Sarah Kenwood. But I don't remember anyone texting me while we were there."

I thought for a minute. "Did you have your phone on you?" I asked.

"Yeah, of course. I... uh wait," Jace hesitated, then his expression cleared. "Lucy... I probably set it on the desk where we were keeping score. I usually do that."

"So, what are you saying?" My mind was doing cartwheels. "You think Sarah was the one texting Sukie?"

"I-I don't know. Why would she do that?"

"Because she liked you, and she knew that Sukie did

too." I was suddenly sure that that was what had happened. "She wanted to eliminate the competition."

It all made sense, really—why Jace had gone from being normal and nice to being vicious and mean in the space of two days. Why I couldn't reconcile the person who sent Sukie those texts with the decent guy I knew from the AO. The person texting with Sukie that day in my bedroom, the one she'd been hating for the past two years, *wasn't* Jace. It was one of her new cheerleader friends, Sarah Kenwood.

"Wow," he said now.

"Yeah," I agreed. "Wow. Would you believe that for the last two years we've been referring to you as 'He Who Shall Not Be Named' because Sukie's still so angry about the whole thing?"

"He Who Shall Not..." Jace repeated the words.

"...Be Named," I finished for him. "So I suppose that now she and her new friends have some terrible nickname for me too."

Jake thought for a minute. "Maybe it's 'She Who Dates the Evil One,'" he suggested.

I smiled in spite of myself. "Or 'She Who Projectile Vomits.'"

We both laughed, but I stopped a moment later when he leaned across the blanket and caressed my cheek with his fingers. "How about 'She Who Looks Beautiful Under the Stars'?" he said softly.

I opened my mouth to reply with "She Who Has Mustard Breath" as a sort of warning, but then he was kissing me and I figured he already knew that. As first kisses go, it was pretty spectacular, and how could it not be? There we were, on top of the world, under an inky night sky filled with stars winking their approval down at us.

No matter what happened, even if I turned out like Nana Lucy in the end, I knew *this* was something I'd remember for the rest of my life.

BY AIR MAIL
PAR AVION
Royal Mail

Worldwide
postcard

The Alamo

May 15th

Howdy Pardner,
    Our bus finally rolled into
Texas, and I have two words for
you: "hot" and "dry." We've
toured the Mission Trail and
the Alamo; the guide wanted
us to imagine the battle, but
all I could think of was getting
back on the air-conditioned bus!
    Remember this: I love you!
        Nana Lucy
P.S. People who live in Texas
must be part salamander!

LOND

PICCADILLY CIRCUS

twenty-five

After Jace brought me home, I managed to make it all the way inside the house without my feet touching the ground. I was about to float down the hallway to my bedroom when a voice from the kitchen brought me back to earth. "Lucy? Did you have a nice time?"

I shook off the last of the stars that were still clinging to my hair and realized that Mom was sitting at the kitchen table.

"Why are you sitting there in the dark?" I reached for the light switch.

"No, don't turn it on," she told me. "Come sit with me."

I made my way across the kitchen, careful not to bump into the island. "How come you're still up?" Mom usually hit the hay by ten, and it was just past midnight.

"It's been a busy night," Mom sighed as I sat down in the chair across from her. "We were all in bed when apparently Nana woke up and decided it was time for *breakfast*. By the time I got out here, she'd fried up all the eggs she could find in the refrigerator, along with enough bacon to feed an army."

I sniffed, realizing that the pleasant aroma hanging in the air was, indeed, bacon. "But...why? Did she have a dream or something?"

Mom sighed. "When we finally got her to stop and talk to us, it turned out that she thought she was back on the farm, cooking a big country breakfast for the farm hands. I don't know who was more upset, Nana Lucy or your father, when she couldn't find any buttermilk in the 'icebox.' 'Pa has to have his buttermilk,' she said. 'It's his favorite way to start the day.'"

I felt a tightening in my throat, a familiar feeling lately. "So how did you get her back to reality?"

"I'm not sure we did," Mom admitted. "She finally burned her wrist on the griddle, and I told her that I'd take over. She wouldn't go back to bed until I convinced her that she needed to be fresh for when the men came in for lunch."

"You lied to her?"

"It isn't lying, exactly," Mom said. "It's called 'validation.' I've been reading about it in a book Dr. Thompson recommended."

"Validation" sounded like a scientific term, but it still felt like lying as far as I was concerned. "But isn't the medicine supposed to keep these things from happening?"

"No," Mom said. "The medicine will slow down the progression of the illness, but it doesn't stop it. When we met with the doctor, she told us that Nana Lucy will have periods of confusion, especially later in the day. That has a name, too: 'sun-downing.' And it's not unusual for people with Alzheimer's disease to have trouble sleeping at night, and to get up and wander around, when they're more confused. I guess that's what happened tonight."

It made sense; I was the first one to admit that Nana Lucy had become an increasingly restless bed partner. Some nights I'd just drop off to sleep when suddenly she'd jerk or mutter something that would pull me back to consciousness. When I was really tired, it could be highly annoying.

"Mom," I asked tentatively, "is Nana Lucy going to die from this?" I wasn't sure I wanted to know the answer, but at the same time I couldn't stand not knowing. Especially since I slept with her.

Mom shook her head. "No," she said. "But she may eventually die from a complication of it."

"What do you mean … complication?" It seemed to me that having Alzheimer's was complication enough.

Mom seemed to be considering how to explain it to me. "Dr. Thompson said that as the disease progresses, people forget how to do basic daily activities such as eat or keep moving, and they sort of … waste away. Or they get sick with something else, like pneumonia, when they're too weak to fight it off."

I didn't know what to say. A montage of images flashed across my mind: Nana Lucy's spirited laugh as she beat me at a game of Scrabble, Nana at the airport, beaming at the sight of us lined up waiting for her, Nana smiling proudly whenever she was in town for one of Rachel's piano recitals or Michael's soccer games. "We can't just let this happen, Mom," I sighed, knowing even as I said it that I had no control over it. "Isn't there something else we can do?"

Mom covered my hand with hers. "Hopefully it's all a long way down the road, sweetie. And frankly, if the time comes when she's so confused that she doesn't even know us ... well, I don't think your Nana would want to live anymore anyway, do you?"

I considered this. "No," I said finally.

Mom squeezed my hand, then sat back in her chair with a sigh. "Do you want to hear something weird?"

I nodded, not at all sure that I did.

"The truth is, I've never felt very close to Nana Lucy. Something about her always made me feel ... well, I guess I felt like I didn't measure up in her eyes. Your grandmother comes from a different era, where things were more formal. She spent her adult years running a tight ship; she helped your grandfather at the store every day and still made it home to make lunch for Dad and Carol. Her house was always spotless, and it seemed like every time I visited I'd manage to spill something. She's loosened up a lot. You probably don't remember this, but at Lucy and Sam Kellogg's house, each meal was color-coordinated, with every food group represented."

"Kind of like Martha Stewart," I offered.

"Exactly. And then there was the way she dressed ..." Mom was lost in her memories. "Always the immaculate suits, and coordinated pumps. You'd never know she grew up a farm girl; she acquired style later in life. When I married her perfect son, well ... I always felt like she was looking at me and seeing how imperfect I was. Being around her, I always felt like ... oh, I don't know. Like she could tell that I don't always use bleach on my whites and that sometimes I use boxed cake mix. And I've never mended a pair of underwear in my life. If it gets holes, I just throw it away and buy new."

"Oh Mom." I laughed. "Who mends their underwear?"

Mom raised an eyebrow and sighed.

I considered this. "Why did you feel like she judged you? Did she say things like that to you?"

"Oh, heavens no," Mom said. "She's got too much class to let on if she thought badly of me. She's never less than cordial, but 'cordial' isn't exactly a warm relationship. In all these years, I've just never felt close to her, or ever knew how to relate to her. But since she's been here this time, strangely, I'm finding that she's much more ... approachable, somehow. I'm actually enjoying her charming little stories about growing up on the farm. She seems so much happier when she's talking about those things. Have you noticed?"

I hadn't, but now that I thought about it, I realized Mom was right. Nana Lucy often seemed anxious or worried, but when she was reminiscing about things early in her life, her eyes would soften and the lines of tension in her face would relax. It was almost as if the past felt more manageable and comforting to her than the present.

"Well, anyway," Mom said, "it's just been kind of … nice."

We sat quietly for a moment, reflecting on our own thoughts, before Mom changed the subject. "So, tell me about your evening."

A smile reflexively stretched across my face at the memory of it. "Um, it was nice. Really nice."

Mom smiled back at me. "I can *see* that. Jace seems like a nice boy. What did the two of you end up doing?"

I considered what to tell her. "Oh, we drove around for a little while, then got some food. Then we just talked." It was all true. After the most perfect kiss in the history of the universe, Jace and I had settled onto our backs on the blanket and lost ourselves in the stars as we talked about anything that came into our minds. I'd learned about his two older brothers, Ross and Derek. He'd also had a little sister, Tory, who'd died of leukemia when she was three. Jace's voice cracked when he told me his family still called him 'Ace,' the name Tory called him before she could say 'Jace.'"

"I was ten when she died," he told me. "She'd been in the hospital for a long time, but I still couldn't believe it the day my dad called and said she was gone. Even though we knew she was going to die, I cried until I threw up."

I hadn't been able to look at him as he spoke, for fear that the tears welling in my eyes would leak down the side of my face. "She's probably up there right now watching us," I managed; just then a star shot across the sky, its tail a trail of stardust. "See?"

Jace was quiet for a while, but I could hear him breathing. "Yeah," he said finally, reaching over to take my hand.

"… What's going on with Sukie?" Mom was saying, interrupting my thoughts.

"Uh, well, I don't know exactly." I reached for the bowl of pretzels someone had left on the table. "She's been really moody lately. You know how stubborn she can be."

"Hmm," Mom said, which was her way of telling me that she had more on her mind. She cleared her throat delicately. "Rachel mentioned that Sukie brought back all the things you've left at her house?"

I nodded. Part of me wanted to confess the whole story to Mom so she could reassure me I'd done nothing wrong, but it was late and I'd had a very big day. What I really wanted most was to go to bed and think more about Jace.

Mom was still sitting quietly, waiting for me to say more. "I don't know," I said. "Sukie's just… going through some things. You know, with cheerleading and all that, she's been stressed out. She'll snap out of it. I'm not worried." I hoped my voice sounded more convincing than I felt. To tell the truth, at this particular moment, I didn't really care if Sukie came around or not.

Mom nodded. "Okay," she said. "I was worried that you two had had a fight."

I shrugged. "Nope."

"Well, then, that's good." Mom glanced up at the clock hanging above the sink. "Oh my goodness, it's nearly one in the morning! We'd better get to bed or we'll be the ones making no sense tomorrow."

"Mm-hmm. But before I go to bed ... is there any of that bacon left?"

Mom laughed. "In the refrigerator. But don't eat too much or you won't be able to sleep."

I didn't answer, but I wasn't worried. And sure enough, twenty minutes later I was tucked into bed and fast asleep beside Nana Lucy who was herself, for once, sleeping like a baby.

twenty-six

I woke the next morning to murmuring voices and more good smells coming from the kitchen. Opening my eyes, I saw that Nana Lucy's side of the bed was empty. Since there was sun outside my bedroom window, I figured I didn't have to worry. Snuggling down under the blanket, I let my mind drift back over the date with Jace. I could still remember the feeling of his lips on mine; the thought of it made me smile. The only thing missing was a call to Sukie to relive my first real date in great detail. That, obviously, was out of the question, so I pushed the thought away.

I'd closed my eyes and was pleasantly drifting off again when I heard someone push the door to my bedroom open. "Mother Bear, there's someone sleeping in my bed!" called a familiar voice, breaking through my dreamy state.

"Wha...?" I groggily opened my eyes just as Serena landed on top of me with her full weight.

"Umph," I groaned as the air was squashed out of me. "Get off of me! What are you doing home, anyway?"

Serena giggled and rolled off. "Why so crabby, sweetie?

Aren't you glad to see me?" She threw a heavy leg over my stomach.

"Oof, get off!" I cried, half irritated, half amused. I was fully awake now, and I pushed against her with all my strength so that she almost fell off the bed, laughing. "Seriously," I said, jabbing her once more for good measure. "Why are you here?"

"I got the weekend off, so I wanted to surprise everybody." Serena was doing a summer internship at a law office in Missoula and hadn't been able to come home since her college classes ended.

"Is Kevin here too?" I asked hopefully. Kevin was Serena's boyfriend and a total cutie, even if he was a cowboy and really shy. She'd met him at a rodeo during her first semester at college and they'd been together ever since.

"Nope." She made a face. "He had to go back to the ranch and help his dad with branding."

"Oh. Too bad."

"Mm-hm." She lifted her head and glanced towards the doorway to make sure no one could hear us. Satisfied, she let her head fall back on Nana Lucy's pillow. "So what's the deal with Nana?" she asked in a low voice, turning to look at me. "Is she totally losing it?"

I snuggled deeper into my cozy blanket nest. "Well, kind of," I sighed. "At first she seems mostly normal, but if you're with her for a while you'll see. She gets mixed up about things. When she got here, she was telling us this story about being a little girl dancing in a ballet, and I swear it was something she'd seen in a movie on the Classic Movie Channel."

"Wow, really? Doesn't it make you a little nervous sleeping in here with her?"

"Not really." I laughed. "Why, do you think she's going to strangle me in my sleep?"

"You never know … you better start sleeping with one eye open, just in case."

I pulled the pillow from behind my head and whacked her with it. "Maybe Nana should worry about sleeping with *me!*"

"Girls, are you coming?" Mom called from the kitchen, "I've got breakfast casserole." So *that* was what Mom had done with Nana Lucy's late-night culinary achievement.

"Oops, that reminds me." Serena said. "Mom sent me in here to tell you to come have breakfast."

Dad, Rachel, and Nana Lucy were already gathered expectantly around the table when Serena and I arrived in the kitchen. Mom set the steaming casserole dish in the middle of the table. "Mmm," Dad said. "My favorite."

"Since everyone slept late, I decided we'd skip breakfast and go straight to brunch," Mom announced.

"It looks delicious, Margo." Nana Lucy reached for the glass of orange juice Mom had set by her place. "I slept well last night but I still feel a bit tired, for some reason."

"What happened to your hand, Nana?" Rachel asked. We all looked at Nana Lucy, who turned her hand to look and nearly spilled her orange juice. I suddenly remembered Mom saying that Nana had burned her hand when she was cooking.

"Why, my heavens, I don't know." Nana looked baffled. "I don't remember anything about it."

"I'll put some aloe on it after we've finished eating," Mom told her breezily. "I keep an aloe vera plant growing just for things like that. Now could someone pass me a napkin, please?"

I wasn't sure why Mom didn't just remind Nana Lucy about the cooking, but I figured it was something that she must have read about in her book. I poured some orange juice into the glass at my place and helped myself to a slice of toast.

"So, Lucy, I hear you had a hot date last night," Serena said casually, causing my knife to pause en route to the butter.

"A *hot* date, was it?" Dad asked, raising an eyebrow. "What does that mean, exactly?"

I rolled my eyes, even though I could feel my cheeks growing warm. "It was just a regular date," I told him, aiming a kick at Serena under the table. "A very nice, regular date with a nice, regular guy."

"Hmm," Dad responded noncommittally.

"He was totally *hot,* Serena," Rachel said, prompting Mom to give her a look. It was pretty much a foregone conclusion that my little sister had lain awake last night, trying to imagine what Jace and I might be doing on our date.

Unfortunately, this time I couldn't keep the smile from my face. "Yeah, he's pretty hot," I agreed, making Rachel beam.

"Courting was very different when I was a girl," Nana Lucy remarked. "If two young people started keeping company with each other on a regular basis, it was generally expected that they would marry."

"Oh, good God!" I sputtered.

"You're getting *married?*" Rachel asked, alarmed. Serena choked on her juice, and even Mom giggled.

"*No!*" I assured everyone loudly. This conversation had gone on too long, as far as I was concerned. "Can someone please pass me the toast? Please?"

After brunch was over and we'd helped Mom with the dishes, Serena mentioned that she needed to pick up a few things downtown and invited me to come along. "You can even drive," she offered.

"Cool." We hadn't been that close when she was living at home, but since Serena had gone off to college, she seemed to treat me like more of a friend when she came home. I threw on some shorts and a T-shirt and met her outside, where her blue Mazda was parked in the driveway.

"Are you sure you want me to drive?" I was suddenly reluctant. I hadn't had *that* much experience.

"Of course," Serena said, tossing me the keys. With no further ado, she climbed into the passenger seat and rolled down the window.

I got in and put on my seat belt. After turning the key in the ignition, I positioned my hands at ten and two on the steering wheel and backed the car carefully down the driveway onto the street.

Serena didn't seem to be worried about my driving abilities; she didn't even seem to be paying attention. "Wow, the more things change, the more they stay the same," she marveled, taking in the sights as we headed downtown. "It's funny how when I lived here I couldn't wait to get out, but now everything looks so ... nice."

"It's just that it's familiar," I told her. "Like a security blanket. Even though it's all ragged and stained, it still makes you feel better just knowing you can still wrap it around you once in a while."

Serena laughed. "You're probably right."

Five minutes later I was guiding the Mazda into a prime parking place in Town Square. "How'd I do?" I got out and tossed the keys to Serena.

"You passed," she said, catching them. Her eyes traveled beyond me. "Hey... isn't that your friend's dad?"

I turned to follow her gaze and saw that indeed it was. Mr. Hollister was two rows away, settling grocery bags into the trunk of his car. "Uh, yeah." I hoped he wouldn't see us.

Too bad for me: a second later, he slammed the trunk and saw us. "Well, hi girls," he called, waving. "Beautiful day, isn't it? What are you two up to this morning?"

There was nothing for me to do but shut my car door and wander towards him.

"Hi," I said. "Serena's in town for the weekend and she needs to pick up a few things."

He smiled, his handsome face crinkling. "There's no place like home, but you don't realize that until you leave, right?"

Serena laughed. "You can say that again."

We made a little more small talk, and I was ready to be on our way when Mr. Hollister said something out of left field.

"Say, Lucy," he asked cheerfully, "I know you're busy

right now, but do you have a couple minutes? Nothing serious; I just wanted to talk to you about something."

The bottom fell out of my stomach. "Uh…I guess so."

I looked at Serena, who hesitated, seeing my face. "Sure, no problem," she said finally. "I'll just run in Osco and get my stuff. Meet you back here?"

"Great," I responded faintly, my mouth dry. Was Sukie's dad going to yell at me right here in the Town Square parking lot?

Mr. Hollister didn't say anything for a minute as we watched Serena walk away. He leaned back against his sedan and propped one leg up on the fender. I relaxed a little; he hardly looked ready to attack. "So how've you been, Lucy?" he asked finally. "Barb and I were just saying that we haven't seen you around the house for a while."

I nodded, feeling awkward. "I know," I admitted. "I've been, uh, busy, I guess. Work, and stuff at home…"

Mr. Hollister made an expression like he was just remembering something. "Ah, yes. Sukie mentioned your grandmother had come to stay for a while."

I nodded, wondering what else Sukie might have told him about me. "Yeah," I replied, "it's been kind of different."

"Dementia is a disease that's tough on everyone," he agreed. "It's like losing someone you care about when they're still right there with you."

"That's kind of true, actually." I was distracted by the

idea for a moment, so he caught me off guard with his next comment.

"Lucy, the reason I'm glad to run into you is that I've been a little worried about things with you and Sukie. I know the two of you have had some sort of argument."

"Sukie told you about it?" I asked, my face growing hot. It made me mad to be put on the spot, having to explain like this, actually. I really didn't think I was the one who'd brought things to this point; if only Sukie had let me talk to her, everything could have been explained a long time ago.

"She told me a little bit about it," Mr. Hollister said. "Something about a boy you've been dating."

"It was *one* date," I clarified. "The other time was just... well, it wasn't a date."

Mr. Hollister nodded as if he understood, when I knew he couldn't possibly.

"Sukie just needs to listen to me." I leaned against the car beside him. "The whole thing is a big tangle of misunderstandings now, and it's totally not what she's thinking it is." I suppose I could have gone into the whole explanation for Mr. Hollister's benefit, but I didn't feel like I wanted to.

"Hmm," he said finally, looking thoughtful. "Well, if you say that, I believe you."

Why would I lie?

"Listen, Lucy, I'll see if I can convince Sukie to hear you out. She may still need to stew about things for a while, though; I'm sure I don't need to tell you that she's a stubborn one. Guess she got that from her mother."

He laughed, and I did too. "That would be great," I said.

Mr. Hollister nodded. "You two have been best friends for too long to let some guy come between you."

"Yeah." It sounded easy when he said it, but I knew things were more complicated than that. It wasn't just the issues about Jace that had to be resolved, I realized suddenly. I had my own hard feelings towards Sukie: the way she'd abandoned me after she made cheerleading and not thought about how that might make me feel, the fact that she'd so easily tossed our friendship aside when she thought I was seeing Jace. I kept coming back to that moment when I'd fallen into the Hollisters' shrubbery and Sukie had turned and gone inside, leaving me to pick myself up. Even if Sukie and I were able to clear things up, I wasn't sure that it would be so easy to put the past behind us.

So much had already happened. I'd seen my grandmother becoming someone other than the person I'd known and loved all my life, and I'd discovered that a person I'd despised for two years was someone completely different than I'd thought he was. And most importantly of all, I'd learned that a best friend is not someone you can necessarily count on.

"Well, I suppose I'd better get going." Mr. Hollister interrupted my thoughts by standing up straight again. "I've got frozen food in some of those bags."

"Yeah, okay," I said numbly. "Tell ... um, take care." I'd been about to say "tell Sukie hello" but decided against it.

To tell the truth, I wasn't sure now what I *wanted* to happen between me and Sukie.

"You, too." Mr. Hollister nodded, already heading around to get in his car. I heard the engine ignite as I started off towards Osco Drug after Serena.

When I heard him drive away behind me, I didn't even turn to wave goodbye.

Worldwide
postcard

San Francisco cable cars

November 4th

Dear Lucy,

San Francisco is a fascinating place to visit; I've ridden on the very cable car shown on the front of this card! Today we're touring the Napa Valley and having lunch at a winery; we're all looking forward to it, especially Rose (she's a bit of a lush).

Remember this: I love you!

Nana Lucy

LOND

PICCADILLY CIRCUS

Dear Lucy

twenty-seven

Serena stayed through the weekend, then headed back across the state line into Montana. "Please greet Kevin for us," Mom told her, hugging her goodbye before she left.

"I will," Serena said, reaching to give Nana Lucy a hug too. "Bye, Nana. Take care of yourself. I'll be back for the Fourth of July, and next time I'll bring Kevin."

"It was good to see you, dear," Nana Lucy told her. "But I'm probably going to be heading home soon, so I probably won't see you again until Christmas."

Serena looked surprised and opened her mouth to say something, but Mom cut her off. "Well, you just never know what life will bring, do you, Nana?" I felt funny knowing that, in fact, everyone but Nana Lucy knew what life would bring her: an airplane ride to Aunt Carol's house in Wisconsin. Before she got Alzheimer's, no one would have ever thought to deceive Nana Lucy like this. I hoped the day never came when everyone around me was making plans for my life behind my back, and lying to me about them.

I said all this to Mom later, after Serena left, when

Nana Lucy had gone to take Scooby for a walk with Rachel. Mom sighed unhappily. "It's not lying, Lucy. It's just putting the truth on hold for right now. There's no point in upsetting her when the future is still uncertain."

"But it's not uncertain," I insisted. "The plans have pretty much already been put into place. You said yourself that Carol was going to get rid of Nana Lucy's apartment. Even if the medicine works and she doesn't get any worse, there won't be a place for her to go back to. The least you could do would be to tell her what's going to happen. How can she adjust to the idea if she doesn't even know about it?"

Mom considered what I was saying, then sighed. "I suppose you're right," she admitted. "I never really thought of it that way. Maybe...well, I guess I've been avoiding the whole issue because I know she's going to be upset. It's been easier to push the discussion off into the future."

"Well, it just seems kind of...disrespectful," I told her. "I feel like we're treating Nana Lucy like a child who's going to the doctor for a shot. We figure if we don't tell her until she gets there, it won't hurt quite as much. But it's not fair, because she's not a child, and it's going to hurt whenever you tell her."

Mom looked thoughtful. "Maybe you're right, Lucy. I tell you what: I'll talk it over with your dad and see what he thinks. We've got to have the conversation at some point. Maybe it's better to do it sooner rather than later."

The phone rang, interrupting our discussion, and I ran to get it. In spite of any reservations I might have, a little part of me still hoped that maybe it was Sukie, calling to say she'd talked to her father and we needed to talk. After we'd cleared things up and I'd told her that the stuff with Jace was all a misunderstanding, we'd laugh about it and then she'd want to hear all about my date with Jace. We'd squeal with glee over the good parts, and … "Hello?" I said eagerly, "Kellogg residence."

"Hey, Lucy." Jace's deep voice came across the wire, tickling my ear. "It's me: 'He Who Was Hoping You Were Home.'"

I felt a smile spread across my face, even though it wasn't Sukie calling. "Hey, what're you up to?"

"Not much. I went to Minot with my dad yesterday to look at cars. Bonnie's on her last legs."

"Really? She seems okay to me."

"Yeah, but the truth is, her transmission could go at any time. I've been trying to keep her limping along until I could save up enough to buy something new, but Dad said that he'd loan me the money now if I found the right car."

"Well that's exciting," I replied, secretly disappointed to know that Bonnie was on her way out. Could *nothing* ever stay the same?

"I guess so," Jace agreed. "It'll be a bummer to send Bonnie to the junkyard."

"Yeah, no kidding. So, did you and your dad find a replacement?"

"No, we were really just looking. How about you? Did you do anything fun?"

I told Jace about Serena's surprise visit. "We've gotten a lot closer since she went to college," I added when I'd finished the story.

"I know what you mean," he said. "My older brothers used to pound the hell out of me before they moved out. Now they're a lot nicer. Derek even left Bonnie to me when he joined the Marines."

"That *is* nice." Suddenly, Mr. Hollister's words came back to me:

You two have been best friends for too long to let some guy come between you.

As if he were reading my mind, Jace asked about Sukie. "So, have you heard anything from 'She Who Hates My Guts'?"

I giggled in spite of myself. "No, but I was thinking maybe I should try and talk to her again. I just know that if she heard the whole story, she might change her mind."

"Yeah," Jace agreed hopefully. "She'd see that I'm not such an evil bastard after all." He fell silent for a moment. "Listen, you said she's your, you know, best friend … if it's going to cause problems for you, maybe we shouldn't see each other anymore. I'd be bummed, but I'd understand."

I swallowed hard. "I don't really know what to say," I admitted, not wanting to tell him about Mr. Hollister's comments along the same lines. "Sukie *is* my best friend— or at least she was—and I really hope we can work things out. But if we can't, well, I guess that's going to be because that's what she wants, in which case there's not much I can do about it."

"Besides," I added, thinking out loud, "if she's really my friend, she'd be happy that I'm happy, no matter what. That's how I felt when she made cheerleading and I didn't." As the words came out of my mouth, I felt another surge of self-righteous anger. I *had* been genuinely happy for Sukie when she got what we both wanted, even though I was disappointed for myself. Why shouldn't she put her own pride aside for my happiness, as any true friend would?

"As a matter of fact," I told Jace, "I think I'll give her a call right now. If this is going to be a permanent thing, I might as well find out."

"Right now?"

"Yep. Right now."

"Okay then," he said. "Well, good luck. Let me know what happens."

"Thanks." I hung up and dialed Sukie's number before I could give it any more thought. She answered the phone on the third ring.

"Hello?" she said. In the background, I could hear the sounds of a television program.

"It's Lucy," I declared boldly. "I think we need to talk."

There was a silence. "All right," she said after a moment. "What do you want to say?"

"First of all," I told her, "I think you owe me an apology."

"I owe *you* an apology?" She repeated incredulously. "That's completely ridiculous! Sarah Kenwood told me that Jace Turner has been working at AO since before school even let out. You've been seeing him for months and didn't even bother to tell me. In fact, I can only think that you decided not to, right?"

I was silent, knowing it was true. This wasn't really how I'd planned to start off the conversation.

"Then," Sukie went on, "when cheerleading took up

so much of my time you got jealous, and wanted to hurt me. You saw an opportunity and you took it."

My mouth was literally hanging open, I was so flabbergasted. I could see how Sukie was thinking I'd betrayed her even more when she found out I hadn't told her Jace was working with me, but to hear that she'd manipulated the details and events in her mind to make it look like an act of jealous revenge made me sick. And furious.

"Well, obviously I've hit the nail on the head." She apparently took my silence as an admission of guilt. "So, maybe it's you who owes *me* an apology, don't you think?"

"You've got it all twisted!" I sputtered, "Maybe I didn't tell you right away when Jace showed up at the AO, but not because I was trying to keep it from you for any bad reason." I tried to think of how to explain the "good" reasons and was horrified when I suddenly couldn't come up with any. "I was afraid that you'd react like this," is what I finally said. "That you'd get completely irrational and freak out, and put all sorts of pressure on me to treat him like crap."

"So you decided to go to the other extreme and become his girlfriend?"

"No ... I don't know. The point is that none of this was done to hurt you. I can't believe you'd think I'd be so ..."

Suddenly I heard voices in the background calling Sukie. "Look," she said, "I've got to go. Fiona and Sarah are here to pick me up; the cheerleaders are having a car wash this afternoon."

"Oh, and speaking of your good friend, *Sarah*," I began, but she'd already hung up. "She's the one who sent you those texts!" I hollered to no one, and crashed the phone receiver back into its cradle. I'd never felt so angry and frustrated; it was even worse than before I'd made the call.

"Good heavens, what's all the ruckus?" I turned to see Nana Lucy standing in the doorway. She was wearing the pretty outfit she'd had on the day she arrived, but her skirt was twisted around sideways. She'd applied eye makeup in a bright turquoise shade, clear up to her eyebrows, and was clutching her purse.

"Are you going somewhere, Nana?" I asked her tiredly. My entire body suddenly felt weak, as if the conversation with Sukie had drained all the energy out of me.

"I was hoping you could give me a ride down to the police station," she said. "I-I need to report some things that have been stolen from my purse."

I didn't bother to tell Nana Lucy that I couldn't drive her anywhere. "What's missing?" I sighed. "Maybe you misplaced it."

"No, my Estée Lauder 'Pretty Pansy' lipstick is gone," she said urgently, glancing around as if she might spot the thief escaping. "And my wallet's missing, too. I put them both in my purse this morning, and now they're gone. I didn't want to worry you all, Lucy, but there have been people coming into the house and taking things for weeks. I'd hoped they'd just take what they wanted and leave us alone, but they don't seem to want to let up. It's time to notify the authorities!"

I took a deep breath and regarded my agitated grandmother. No matter what was going on in my personal life right now, it was nowhere near as upsetting as it would be to believe that strangers were stealing my things.

"How about if you just sit down and relax for a few minutes," I said. "I'll go back to the bedroom and get my shoes on and then we can go." I was halfway hoping that by the time I returned, Nana Lucy would have calmed down and I could distract her with a game of Yahtzee. *Or maybe checkers*, I amended. Given the state I was in, the sound of dice skittering noisily onto the table might send me over the edge.

"Fine," Nana said, momentarily placated. "I'll just wait here. But please hurry, dear; the sooner the police can start working on the case, the better." She perched on the couch, her purse on her lap, to wait for me.

I went back to the bedroom and took my time finding my shoes. The longer I was gone, the greater the likelihood that Nana Lucy would forget about the whole thing, I told myself. Stalling for a few more minutes, I began searching the room for her things, looking on shelves, in shoes, and in the pockets of her clothes.

I found her wallet in the nightstand drawer on her side of the bed, along with a can of soup, two cookies wrapped in a napkin, and a bag of miniature carrots that were obviously long past their expiration date. The lipstick was in Nana's cosmetic bag in the bathroom.

"Look, Nana," I said, returning to the living room with the "stolen" items. "You must have put them away yourself and forgotten about it."

Nana Lucy was looking impatient. I thought she'd be relieved to see I'd found her things, but instead her eyes narrowed. "Oh, they're crafty, all right," she muttered. "Those scoundrels must have known I was about to report them." She snatched the items from my hand and dropped them into her purse, then snapped it securely shut. "I'm not going to fall for it, and I hope you won't either," she commanded sternly, getting to her feet and heading out of the living room.

As she left I heard her muttering something about "arming herself," and knew that couldn't be good. With a sigh, I went to find Mom.

twenty-eight

"I know the psychiatrist said it was a mild antipsychotic, but it's still strong medication," Dad said, scowling into the rearview mirror. We were on our way home from the doctor's office where Nana Lucy had been given her first dose, and already she had dozed off between me and Rachel in the back seat. "Look at how groggy it's making her."

"That's a little more than groggy," observed Rachel, regarding Nana Lucy's slack features and half-open mouth. "She looks dead."

"Rachel!" Mom scolded.

"She may just be tired because she's not sleeping well at night," I volunteered, hoping it would make Dad feel better. Judging from his heavy sigh, I knew I hadn't been successful.

"I know it's scary to have her on so much medication, Bruce," Mom said, reaching over to rub Dad's shoulder as he drove. "But you have to imagine how anxious it would make you if you believed strangers were coming into the house and stealing your things. Yesterday, she even told me she thought Michael had taken some of her shoes and sold them to make money for drugs. When I reminded her that Michael was off at soccer camp, and that he certainly didn't use drugs, I could see she didn't believe me. It's only a matter of time before she starts thinking we're *all* in on some kind of conspiracy against her."

I looked over at Nana Lucy, her body drooping in sleep. It was becoming harder and harder to imagine she'd ever been the witty, sharp-minded person I'd known most of my life. Mom had managed to get her to bathe and brush her teeth before the appointment, but her hair was a rat's nest and in spite of the medication, it was getting harder and harder to convince her to keep up with basic hygiene. It was becoming obvious to all of us that the medication to slow the progression of her dementia wasn't working.

"I can't imagine what might have happened if we hadn't had her come to stay with us when we did." Mom looked back over the seat at Nana Lucy. "She could have started a fire with the stove, wandered out into the city … anything. Thank God she had good friends who cared enough about her to call Carol."

Dad didn't say anything, just kept his eyes on the road. He so often seemed cranky or distracted these days, and I'd noticed he seemed to be spending even more time away from home than usual. It occurred to me to wonder what it must be like to watch your mother slowly slipping away; I couldn't imagine how strange it would be to see the person who seemed to have all the answers throughout your life slowly becoming as helpless and dependent as a child.

"If she's still with us in the fall," Mom said, "we're

going to have to get someone to come in and stay with her during the day. The kids will be at school and no one will be able to watch her to make sure she's safe while I'm at work." Mom was planning to start working at Rachel's school as an aide. Now she paused delicately for a moment. "Or..." she said, "there's always Vista Manor."

The vehicle swerved slightly and I caught my breath, watching Dad's shoulders tense. "I will not have my mother in a place like that," he vowed. "She would never want that... *never!*"

"Do you think she'll be all that aware that's where she is?" Mom asked. "To tell you the truth, Bruce, sometimes I'm not sure she even knows where she's at when she's at our house."

Dad didn't say anything, and we drove the rest of the way in silence that was punctuated occasionally by sleep murmurs emanating from Nana Lucy. When we got home, Dad stalked into the house, leaving Mom to wake up Nana and help her inside. By unspoken agreement, Rachel and I stayed outside. If there was going to be an argument between Mom and Dad, neither one of us wanted to be around to hear it.

"What's Vista Manners?" Rachel asked, as soon as Mom and Nana Lucy were inside.

"Vista *Manor*," I corrected her. "It's a nursing home on the other side of town. Or not a nursing home, exactly; it's really more of a place for people who are confused like Nana Lucy."

"What do they do to them there?" Rachel wanted to know. "Something bad?"

"No," I said. "It's just a place where people can do what they want, but still be safe." I knew about Vista Manor because we'd visited it for our Occupational Living class, and because a couple girls I knew had jobs there as nursing assistants. Even though it had a nice, homelike atmosphere when we visited, I remembered that there was an old man who was pacing around, wearing a jacket and hat. As we were waiting to begin our tour, he'd approached our group. "Are you girls waiting for the bus?" he asked. We told him that we weren't, and one of the girls had started to explain that we were a group of high school students. Before she could finish, however, he'd interrupted her. "Because if you are," he advised, "it's a lo-o-o-o-ong wait."

"He's been waiting for that bus for a year and a half," one of the aides confided to me in passing. "Says he's got a job interview in Bismarck on Monday."

"Oh," I replied, confused. "Does he really?"

The aide raised her eyebrows at me and shook her head. "Don't worry, George," she told the old man, patting him on the shoulder. "The bus is running a little behind today, but you'll still get there in plenty of time."

"Ah," George had responded, looking relieved. He settled down on a nearby couch and dozed off. When we came back through the main room after our tour, he was gone. I presumed he'd gone off to his room for a rest, or had given up and decided to try some other form of transportation.

"It's kind of like a house, only bigger and more open," I told Rachel now. "The residents all eat their meals around a big table, family style, and there are activities to keep them busy. Things that they still remember how to do, like folding towels or sorting nuts and bolts. Oh, and there are pets there too, dogs and birds. They call them 'therapy animals' because having them around is soothing for the people."

"Why not cats?" Rachel wondered. For as long as Scooby had been part of our family, Rachel had still always longed for a kitten.

"Think about it, Rach,'" I told her. "You can have dogs and birds together, but you can't have dogs and cats, or birds and cats. The cats would cause problems both directions."

"Oh ... I see." She looked disappointed at cats being eliminated from the equation once again. "I guess a lot of people are allergic to cats, too."

"Right."

By late afternoon, Nana Lucy was alert enough to play a game of canasta with Mom, Rachel, and Dad, and I went off to work feeling much better about things. It didn't last long, however. The first person I saw was Donna, looking frazzled as she buzzed past me with a tray full of food.

"Lucy," she said when she came back my way, "we've got problems. Frank broke up with Cherilyn this morning. He's hiding downstairs in the office and she's been crying in the bathroom ever since she got here. I've been able to cover all her tables so far, but she's going to have to get her butt out here before the dinner or I'm going to go in there and kick it for her. These customers are running me ragged; could you go talk to her before you start your shift?"

"Uh, sure," I agreed, not sure at all what kind of wisdom

a sixteen-year-old girl who'd never even had a boyfriend until recently would be able to impart to a grown woman who'd just been dumped.

"*This* is why workplace romances are a bad idea," muttered Donna over her shoulder as she hurried off towards the kitchen to pick up her next order.

I headed slowly towards the women's restroom, glancing at Jace through the kitchen window as I went. He was talking to Lupe, but paused to smile and wave when he saw me. I'd meant to call him back after I'd spoken with Sukie, but then Nana Lucy had asked to be taken to the police station and I'd never gotten a chance.

I didn't know what I'd find inside the bathroom. At first it appeared empty. I wondered whether Donna had been confused, but then I heard a snuffling sound from the farthest stall.

"Cherilyn?" I called uncertainly. "It's me … Lucy. Is that you in there?"

There was a cough and then Cherilyn's voice floated over the stall door. "Y-y-yeah," she hiccuped. "I'm in h-here. I th-thought I'd be okay to come to work, but I was wrong."

I took a deep breath. "Donna said that you and Frank broke up, huh?" There didn't seem to be any point in beating around the bush.

Her only answer was a shuddering sob, broken by a hiccup so sharp it sounded painful.

"I'm sure it seems awful right now," I told her, "but it will get better, I promise."

"How am I supposed to come to work?" Cherilyn

asked. "When I know that Frank's right downstairs? I can't quit, either. I need this job."

I didn't have an answer for that. "Why did he break up with you?" I asked.

There was a sniffling pause before the door to Cherilyn's stall swung open. "He didn't break up with me," she said, blowing her nose as she came out. "I broke up with him." Her face was blotchy and her eyes were red-rimmed.

"Really? I thought... Donna said... "

Cherilyn threw her used tissue in the garbage can next to the sink. "I'm letting everyone think that he broke up with *me*, because he's the manager. I don't want him to be embarrassed to have been dumped by a waitress. He's a great guy, and he doesn't deserve th-that... " At this endorsement, her face collapsed and fresh tears sprouted from her eyes.

I was puzzled. "But if you think he's so great, then how come you broke up with him?"

Cherilyn had gone back into the stall to grab a fresh handful of toilet paper, and now she emerged, wiping her eyes. "You're probably too young to understand it, Lucy," she sighed. "It's complicated. The fact is, Frank's a lot younger than I am, and he's never had any kids or been married. He says he wants to marry me and take care of me and my kids, but the more I thought about it, the more I realized that it wasn't fair of me to pull him into such a complicated situation. My oldest, Bobby, is having trouble with fighting in school, and my daughter has learning disabilities. Vincent, my littlest, has ADHD. And their dads are both criminals, obviously. Frank... he comes from a nice family and has never had to deal with anything like this. It's just too messy, and I know that eventually ... "

"So you broke up with Frank because ... you care about him *too much?*" I asked, surprised. Seriously, sometimes adults are too crazy for me.

"Uh-huh," she sniffled. "I l-l-love him. Besides, he'd probably get sick of all the drama and break up with me somewhere down the road. I just don't know if I could handle that. As soon as I figured all this out, I just figured there's no reason not to just get it over with. But I didn't know I'd feel so *t-t-terrible* ... " Cherilyn put her hands over her face and shook with sobs.

"Cherilyn," I said slowly, "did you tell Frank the reason why you were breaking up with him?"

"Of course not. If I did, he'd only argue with me and tell me I was being ridiculous," she replied. "He'd say that he doesn't care about any of that. And that he loves me and wants to be with me and the kids forever."

I still didn't get it. "So ... what if it's true?"

Cherilyn didn't answer at first. "I don't know," she said finally. "I guess maybe I'm doing it for his own good. If we did get married and he ended up regretting it, I don't think I could live with myself."

We were silent for a minute. Cherilyn was leaning against the sink, sniffling and using a corner of toilet paper to blot the mascara from under her eyes.

"Well," I told her finally, "if you ask me, you're not being fair to Frank. He's got as much right to make decisions about his own life as you do. You're kind of treating him like he's a kid who can't decide what's right for himself."

I felt like I was having a repeat performance of the conversation I'd had with Mom a few days ago. What gave anyone the right to make decisions about other people's lives? It seemed to me that the world would be a much simpler place if everyone just worried about themselves.

Cherilyn considered. "Huh," was all she said, but at least she wasn't crying anymore.

"Well, listen, I'd probably better get out there," I told her. "And you should, too. Donna's getting slammed."

Cherilyn nodded. "Okay, well, thanks, Lucy," she said, reaching to give me a hug. "Maybe you're right. You've given me something to think about, anyway."

"No problem." I left her to finish pulling herself together, and headed out to the restaurant.

"Is she doing any better?" Donna asked, breezing past me with a tray full of chip baskets and shallow bowls of salsa.

"Actually, I think she is," I said, grinning. "We had a good talk, and she's thinking things over."

"Well, who would've believed it?" Donna called back over her shoulder. "Forget 'Lucy'; we're changing your name to Dr. Phil!"

Hannibal, Missouri | The Boyhood Home of Mark Twain

June 1st

Dearest Girl,

    Rose, Arlene, and I decided
that we ought not ignore what
our own part of the country
has to offer, so we signed up
for a Mississippi cruise! The
rolling farmland and wild
wetlands we're passing
remind me of my childhood.
We even saw Mark Twain's
boyhood home; Arlene claims
to have dated him, but frankly,
the numbers don't add up.

    Remember this: I love you!

    Nana Lucy

LOND

PICCADILLY CIRCUS

twenty-nine

After the dinner rush ended, Cherilyn disappeared again, and I hoped it meant that she was downstairs straightening things out with Frank. A new waitress, Marie, had come on shift, and I was watching Donna show her the ropes when Jace came around the corner. "Hey, can you go on break?" he asked.

"I think so." I gestured across the room to Donna, asking her to keep an eye out for stragglers while I was gone. She nodded, and I followed Jace outside.

It was cool and quiet behind the restaurant, and I sat down on a bench to rest my feet. After being on them for three hours straight, I could understand a bit of what Donna and Cherilyn complained about. Jace sat down next to me and stretched his legs out in front of him. "So, were you able to patch things up with Sukie?"

"Well, I called her like I said I was going to. At first I thought it was going to go all right, but then somehow ... I don't know, things got even worse."

Jace looked sympathetic. "Sorry about that." He

reached over and took my hand, sending thrilling little shivers up my arm.

"That's okay." I sighed. "The way she's acting is ridiculous. All that jumping around must have joggled something loose in her brain."

"That's probably it." Jace smiled, rubbing the back of my hand with his thumb in a way that was both comforting and kind of sexy.

"As far as I'm concerned," I declared, "she can stay mad if she wants to. I haven't done anything wrong, and I'm not the one acting insane." My voice sounded firm and convincing, as if I really didn't care whether or not I ever talked to Sukie again.

Jace looked at me carefully. "So … does that mean we can go out again?"

"I guess so." I nodded, then smiled. "If you want to, that is." I thought of what Cherilyn had said. "Maybe you're getting sick of all this drama."

Now it was Jace's turn to smile. "Well, no guy likes drama. But in this case, it's worth it. How about tonight after work? I could pick you up at your house again. I know a great place where we could go shoot some pool."

"I'm terrible at pool, but that sounds fun." I felt my face grow warm with pleasure. I was already looking forward to kissing him again; that alone would make being humiliated at pool well worth it.

"All right, then," Jace said. "It's a date." He stretched, then stood up. "I should probably get back inside before Lupe comes looking for me. I told him it would be quick."

"Yeah, me too. Do you think we'd get too much crap if we both went in through the kitchen?"

"Like I said." Jace grinned. "You're worth it."

I was still smiling to myself when I arrived back at the hostess station. "Wow, you really *are* Dr. Phil," Donna said. "I just took Marie downstairs to show her where to restock the napkins and we caught Frank and Cherilyn making out like teenagers."

I smiled even bigger. "It was simple," I told them, feeling proud in spite of myself. "I just laid it out plain for Cherilyn; actually, I think I told her exactly what she wanted to hear."

Donna rolled her eyes at the new waitress, Marie, who was clearly scandalized by whatever it was that she'd seen in the basement. "Kids these days," she told Marie. "They're too wise for their own good."

Marie nodded in dazed agreement.

Suddenly Doug's head came around the corner from the main dining room. "Lucy, Frank says to tell you you've got a phone call downstairs."

"He probably just wants you to come down so he can give you a big raise," Donna said, laughing. "Or maybe he's going to make you assistant manager."

"Yeah, right." Still, I didn't know what to think; I'd never gotten a call on the office phone before. "I'll be right back, I guess." I headed downstairs.

When I got there, I found Frank and Cherilyn in the office, beaming at each other. I was halfway expecting them to start thanking me, but Frank gestured towards the phone on his desk, where the receiver was off the hook. "Call for you," he said without taking his eyes off Cherilyn.

"Thank you," I told him, picking up the receiver and thinking he should really be thanking *me*.

Mom was on the other end of the line. "Oh, Lucy," she said, sounding relieved. "I'm sorry to call you at work, but I wasn't sure what time your shift ended."

"Eight o'clock. Why?"

"Well, as if all this with Nana Lucy isn't enough, we just got a call from Michael's camp counselor. Apparently some of the boys were horsing around on the dock this evening and Michael slipped and hit his head. They've taken him to the hospital with a concussion."

"Oh *no!*"

"Oh yes. They expect him to be okay," Mom assured me, "but they want to keep him in the hospital overnight for observation. Dad and I are going to drive there as soon as you can get home to stay with Nana."

"I'm sure I can leave right now," I told Mom. "I should be home in fifteen minutes."

"Do you want Dad to come and get you?" Mom asked. "Would that be quicker?"

"Probably," I told her, "but I'd better not leave Michael's bike here."

"All right, then," Mom said. "Ride home, but don't try to rush. We don't need another accident."

I agreed to be careful, and hung up. "My parents need me to come home," I explained to Frank, who grudgingly tore himself away from Cherilyn long enough to hear what I had to say. "My brother got a concussion at camp and someone needs to watch my grandma while they go make sure he's okay."

"Of course, Lucy," Frank said, looking concerned. "Keep us posted." He reached over and put a protective arm around Cherilyn as if she, too, were in danger. *Note to self: Blech.*

I headed back upstairs, where I grabbed my purse from its regular place under the counter at the hostess station and ran out the door. I was halfway home before I realized I hadn't told Jace. Oh well, I figured, someone would fill him in. Right now all I could think about was getting home so that my parents could start the long drive to Michael's soccer camp in Wahpeton. It wasn't even July yet, and already it seemed as if the summer had been filled with crises. *What more could possibly happen?* I asked myself. *Things can only get better.*

As so often happens when you feel absolutely certain about something, I would soon be proven wrong about *that.*

thirty

When I came through the front door, Mom was sitting on the sofa, her overnight bag packed and waiting at her feet. "Lucy, I have a huge favor to ask," she said in a low voice. "I'd forgotten that Nana Lucy has a dentist appointment scheduled for tomorrow at two. She's been complaining of her tooth hurting, so I'd hate to cancel it, but I'm worried we won't make it back in time. Do you think you could get her there?"

I raised my eyebrows. "Can I take your car?" I asked brightly. Mom had a little Honda and it was a fun, zippy car to drive.

She sighed and shook her head. "I'm afraid not. It's not that I wouldn't trust you, but Dad took it to the shop this afternoon for a tune-up. It won't be done before we get back."

For a fleeting instant I pictured myself on Michael's bike, careening down the street to Dr. Jones' office with Nana Lucy teetering along on the handlebars. "So how am I supposed to get Nana to the dentist?"

Mom smiled. "Well, I thought maybe you could call a cab. I know it's sort of an unusual solution, but I really couldn't come up with anything else on such short notice."

"Hmm," I said, tapping my finger to my cheek thoughtfully. "Somehow this seems like a good time to bring up the idea of a car..."

"We'll talk about it when we get back." Mom laughed.

Just then Dad came around the corner. "Are we ready? Where's Rachel?"

"I'm right here," Rachel said, coming in the door. She had Scooby on his leash and Nana Lucy was trailing behind. "Sorry I'm not staying, Lucy," she told me brightly. "I just thought that Michael might need me more."

"I'm sure he'll be glad to see you." I knew it was probably more that Rachel needed to see for herself that Michael was all right. Ever since Nana Lucy had arrived and begun noticeably deteriorating, Rachel had become anxious about the rest of us. She was always asking me how I was doing, and if I was feeling okay.

"Well, I guess it's just you and me, Nana," I told her. "We'll hold down the fort."

"Sure we will, dear," Nana agreed. "We'll hold it down."

"Be good, you two," Dad warned with a smile, giving me a hug and Nana a kiss on her papery cheek. "As always, lock the doors, and no wild parties."

I had a momentary flashback to the "wild party" that had gone on the last time Mom and Dad were away. "Don't worry," I told him wholeheartedly. "A wild party is the last thing we're planning."

Nana Lucy smiled sweetly. "Speak for yourself," she

cautioned, waggling her eyebrows suggestively and making us all laugh. I suspected that Nana Lucy's idea of a wild party would be spending the evening kicking my butt at some dice game.

"Lucy, could you help me in the kitchen for a moment?" Mom called. Both Nana Lucy and I began to get up, but I was quicker.

"She means me, Nana." Nana Lucy settled back into the couch and turned towards the television, where *Father's Little Dividend* was playing. Scooby jumped onto the couch to curl up beside her, and she stroked him absently with one hand as she watched.

When I got to the kitchen, Mom showed me two orangey-brown pharmacist's bottles with white caps. "These are Nana Lucy's nerve pills," she told me, holding up the smaller bottle. "The psychiatrist said she's supposed to take two before bed to help her sleep. He was hoping that if she could get some better rest, she might not lose touch with reality so easily. She can also have one during the day if she's getting anxious or wound up."

"Okay," I said, peering into the bottle. The pills were small and white, and didn't look like they'd be hard to swallow.

"And this is her memory medication," Mom said, holding up the second bottle. This one was larger, and easy to distinguish from the bottle of nerve pills. "She gets one of these a day, in the morning."

"So it's one of these in the morning and two of the other ones before bed," I clarified. "Got it."

Mom nodded. "Like I said, we'll be home sometime

tomorrow, barring any unforeseen complications. And I'll have my cell phone if you need to get in touch before then."

"Don't worry, Mom," I assured her. "We'll be fine." It wasn't as if Nana Lucy was a toddler, after all. The only thing I was worried about was the cab ride tomorrow; I'd never taken a cab by myself before.

Mom read my mind. "I've written down the number of the cab company," she said, handing me a piece of paper and some bills she'd taken from her purse. "And this should be plenty of money to cover the fare."

I nodded. "Mom," I said, "Don't worry. We'll be fine." I hadn't even had time to change out of my work clothes yet, and I was looking forward to putting on something comfortable and settling in with Nana Lucy to watch television. Maybe we'd even make popcorn and find one of the movies she liked so much.

Dad stuck his head in the back door. "Margo, we'd better get on the road if we want to get there before midnight! Rachel's already waiting in the car."

"Oh, I suppose you're right." Mom kissed me hurriedly and picked up her purse. "You girls have fun," she called to Nana Lucy, who waved back at her without taking her eyes from the television set.

Mom headed out the door, and a moment later Dad was backing the Suburban down the driveway. After they'd driven away, I went and changed into a comfortable T-shirt and a pair of Serena's old pajama pants, then rejoined Nana Lucy on the couch. "I always thought that Spencer Tracy had such charisma," Nana commented, glancing up at me as I sat down. "A lot of the other girls liked the good-looking ones better, like Gary Cooper or Bing Crosby. Not me," she said, shaking her head. "Katharine Hepburn and I thought alike."

"See, now, if you were a teenager today," I told her, "you and Hepburn would be saying he was a hottie."

"A hottie," Nana Lucy repeated, nodding. "Yes, I suppose that's it."

Stanley Banks had just learned that he was about to become a grandfather when our phone rang. I jumped up to answer it. "Hello?"

"Hey," Jace's voice was on the other end of the line. "I just finished my shift and Cherilyn told me that you had to leave because of some sort of emergency. What's going on?"

I explained briefly about Michael's injury. "So I had to come home to stay with my grandma."

"I guess you won't be able to go shoot pool tonight, huh?" I couldn't help but be pleased by the disappointment in his voice.

"I don't think so," I said. "My parents are coming home tomorrow, though, with or without my brother. Can I take a rain check?"

"Sure," Jace said. "I don't have to work tomorrow night."

"Me neither."

"It's a date, then. And if you don't want to play pool, we could do something else. Or nothing... just hang out."

"We'll figure it out." I thought about the comforting pressure of Jace's thumb as he stroked the back of my hand. "Call me tomorrow and we'll decide on a time." I figured I'd better wait until my parents got back from their trip before making any plans.

"Sounds good."

We said goodbye, and I glanced at the clock. It was almost nine, and I wondered whether I should give Nana her sleeping medicine. She looked fully engrossed in the movie, so I decided to wait a little longer.

"Would you like a snack, Nana? I could make us some popcorn."

She looked up from the movie. "Is popcorn bad for the baby?"

Now it was my turn to be confused for a moment. "Oh Nana, the baby is on television. See, it's just a movie you're watching. There's no baby here."

Nana looked puzzled, but then her expression cleared. "Oh my goodness," she said. "I don't know what I was thinking. You're right; there's no baby here. It's on the program."

"Maybe ice cream would be better, anyway," I suggested. "Does that sound good?" I went into the kitchen and moved aside Mom's big ceramic pitcher, full of utensils, that sat in the middle of the counter. I took out two bowls.

"It sounds very nice, dear," Nana was saying. "I'll just visit the ladies' room while you're doing that." She stood up and started towards the kitchen, but when she got to the doorway of the family room she paused. "Which way did you say I should go?"

"It's just down the hallway, Nana," I told her. "See, that first door on the left."

"Oh, yes," Nana said. "Of course."

Just in case, I followed her down the hallway and switched on the bathroom light so she could see, then closed the door to give her some privacy. Nana Lucy seemed more confused tonight than ever. It suddenly occurred to me that maybe this was the "sun-downing" Mom had mentioned.

I had just finished scooping ice cream and was getting out the chocolate topping when I heard Nana Lucy's voice coming from the bathroom.

"Shoo! Get out of here!" she cried, her voice rising with each word. The bathroom door flew open. "Call the police!" Nana hollered. "We've got an intruder!"

I rushed down the hallway towards the bathroom, and nearly collided with her as she came towards me in the dimly lit hallway.

"Good grief, Nana, what's wrong?" I reached over to snap on the overhead light. In the sudden brightness, Nana looked crazy; her hands were dripping with water, and her eyes were as wide and round as if she'd seen a ghost. My own heart was pounding with alarm at being summoned so urgently.

"There's an old lady in there!" Nana Lucy said, her voice shaking as she pointed back towards the bathroom. "I was washing my hands and she came out of nowhere! I tried to chase her off, but she wouldn't go; call the police!"

It took me a minute to realize what must have happened, but I was still nervous about a possible intruder as I peered into the bathroom. As I'd suspected, the bathroom was empty.

"She may be hiding in the tub," Nana warned from the doorway behind me. "She looked like a tricky one."

I pulled back the shower curtain. "Nope," I said. "No one's in there, Nana. You must have chased her away after all."

Nana Lucy sighed with relief. "Well, let's hope she doesn't come back. She scared the daylights right out of me."

"If she does, you just call me and I'll take care of it." My heart was heavy in my chest as I peered across the sink into the mirror. Only now it was a young lady, me, reflected there. Not an old lady with cornflower blue eyes and a cloud of hair that used to shine a rich auburn, but had now faded to dull ginger. The person Nana Lucy had seen in the mirror was herself. Someone who, for the moment, she didn't recognize.

"Come on, Nana," I told her, snapping off the light again. When I took her arm, I could feel the pulse under the papery skin inside her elbow racing. "Let's go have some ice cream and finish the movie. It will make you feel so much better."

"Yes, that does sounds lovely, dear," she agreed, and the possibility occurred to me that perhaps she didn't fully know who I was, either. I realized now that I hadn't heard her use my name all evening.

"And after the movie's over," I told her, "we'll get your nightie on, and then I've got some medicine that will give you a wonderful night's rest. You'll see."

Side by side, the old Lucy and the younger one, we moved bravely down the hall.

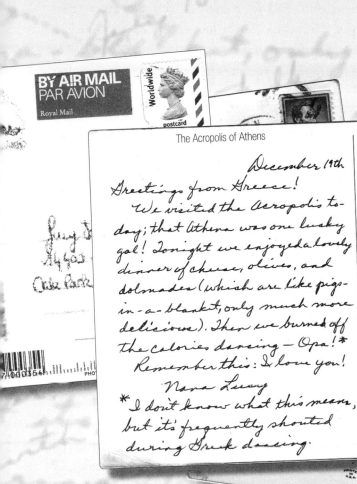

The Acropolis of Athens

December 19th

Greetings from Greece!
We visited the Acropolis to-day; that Athena was one lucky gal! Tonight we enjoyed a lovely dinner of cheese, olives, and dolmades (which are like pigs-in-a-blanket, only much more delicious). Then we burned off the calories dancing — Opa!*
Remember this: I love you!
Nana Lucy
* I don't know what this means, but it's frequently shouted during Greek dancing.

LOND
PICCADILLY CIRCUS

thirty-one

Despite all of the excitement, after I got Nana Lucy tucked into bed and rinsed out our ice cream bowls, I fell into bed beside her and was instantly asleep. Maybe it was the medication that helped her sleep so soundly, but for once I wasn't jostled awake during the night by her fidgeting, crying out, or climbing out of bed to wander through the house like a lost soul.

When I opened my eyes the next morning, I was more refreshed than I could remember feeling since Nana Lucy had arrived. I glanced at the clock on the bedside stand; it was already ten, but the dentist appointment wasn't until two o'clock, so we had plenty of time to spare. I pulled the covers up to my chin and turned on my side, smiling to myself as I remembered my upcoming date with Jace.

After a while, my stomach rumbled, so I decided that I ought to get up and make sure Nana Lucy had found herself some breakfast. I swung my legs over the side of the bed and sat up, noticing Nana Lucy's nightgown lying neatly across the foot of the bed.

"She must have gotten dressed already," I thought, glad she was still able to do that, at least. As I threw on some shorts and a top, I paused to see if I heard or smelled anything suspicious, but nothing seemed amiss. If she had gotten her own breakfast, hopefully Nana Lucy hadn't made too big of a mess. I figured she'd finished up and was probably sitting at the kitchen table, playing game after game of solitaire, or settled on the couch in front of the television watching *The Price is Right*, which for some reason she'd started calling *Truth or Consequences*.

"Nana?" I called, puzzled when I arrived in the kitchen and didn't find her there. In the family room, the television set was silent and Nana was nowhere to be seen. Quickly, I made a search of the other rooms, hoping to find her curled up somewhere with a magazine or a photo album, but she was nowhere to be found. Suddenly, I realized that Nana Lucy wasn't the only one missing from the picture: Scooby wasn't jumping all over me, begging to be fed or taken outside as he normally would be.

"Nana Lucy?" I called again, not wanting to acknowledge what I already knew was true. Neither Nana Lucy nor Scooby were anywhere in the house. "Scooby? Come here boy ... want a treat? Where *are* you guys?"

It occurred to me that they might be as close as the back yard. I hurried out the back door and through the garage into the back yard, but Nana Lucy and Scooby were nowhere to be seen. Coming around to the front, I looked up and down the street, hoping that I'd see them returning from a walk. I wondered whether Nana Lucy knew to put Scooby on a leash, but a check of the garage revealed

Scooby's blue leash still hanging on its usual hook beside the back door. "Oh, Nana," I sighed unhappily. "Where've you gone?"

I went back inside to think. While I was there, it occurred to me that one or both of them might be downstairs, in the basement. I doubted it. Scooby, at least, would have come running up when he heard my voice, and part of me actually hoped they weren't there—Nana had been unsteady lately. A frightening image of her crumpled body lying broken at the foot of the stairs crossed my mind; nervously, I opened the door to the basement, but the light was off and no one answered my calls. I decided to check around down there anyway, and headed down the stairs.

Michael's room is in the basement, so it always smells a little like sweaty socks. "Nana Lucy?" I called when I reached the bottom of the stairs. "Are you down here?"

I hoped she hadn't decided to do a load of laundry; hurrying to the laundry room, I snapped on the light, half expecting to see her sprawled across the floor, blood seeping from her head and laundry strewn everywhere around her lifeless body. To my relief, there was nothing at all to see except a pile of dirty clothes spilling across the floor.

I switched the light off again and sank down on the old musty sofa Michael and his friends liked to hang out on when they watched TV. "Nana Banana, where could you be?" I asked softly. I closed my eyes and concentrated, trying to clear my mind and conjure up a telepathic image of Nana and Scooby. I wasn't even sure they were together, but thinking that they were made me feel better.

A few minutes passed and the only thing I saw was the inside of my eyelids, so I opened my eyes and went back upstairs. I wondered whether I should call Mom, but I wasn't ready to admit the situation was that serious yet. Besides, she was already dealing with Michael's concussion, and I knew there was nothing she could do from so far away. I thought about calling the police, but I wasn't even sure what Nana Lucy had been wearing when she left.

I made one more circuit of the house, but when I still came up empty, I decided it was time to canvas the neighborhood. As I wheeled Michael's bike out of the garage, I saw our neighbor, Mrs. Forrest, watering her petunias. "Hi, Lucy," she called when she saw me. "How's your brother doing? I talked to your dad last night and he sounded pretty worried."

"Mom and Dad went to check on him," I told her. "He's going to be fine, I think."

It occurred to me to ask Mrs. Forrest if she'd seen Nana Lucy, but I wasn't ready to admit I'd lost her. "Um, Scooby's run off again, Mrs. Forrest; did you happen to see him this morning?"

I was hoping that she'd say, *Why, yes, Lucy, I saw your grandmother twenty minutes ago. She was taking Scooby for his walk, told me they were heading east to Spring Lake Park, and would stay on the sidewalk all the way. In fact, she seemed completely alert and oriented, so there's absolutely nothing for you to worry about...*

But, of course, she just smiled at me and shook her head. "I'm sorry, dear. I haven't seen that little rascal this morning. I'll certainly keep an eye out for him though!"

There was nothing for me to do but thank her and hop on my bike for a search-and-recovery mission. I cruised the couple blocks to the park, my heart beating faster as I went, but the only people there were a bunch of daycare kids and their babysitter. The kids were sitting on a blanket in the grass, having a mid-morning snack of cookies and juice boxes, and they all looked up at me when I rode up. "I'm looking for my grandmother," I told the lady handing out cookies. "She took my dog for a walk, and they haven't come back yet. Have you seen anybody like that?"

The lady considered. "What kind of dog is it?" she asked, and I had a moment of hope.

"He's a ... just a brown one," I told her. As I mentioned earlier, Scooby isn't any one kind of dog. "Medium-sized. And my grandmother has red hair. Or she used to have red hair, but now it's kind of strawberry blonde, I guess. In fact she might not even be with my dog; I'm just guessing that they're together. So even if you've seen someone who looks like her ..."

The lady went back to handing out cookies. "No," she said, "we haven't seen anyone like that since we've been here, have we kids?"

"Uh-uh," responded the children, several with cookie crumbs falling out of their mouths.

My hopes sank. "All right," I sighed. "Thanks anyway." I was ready to ride away when I thought to give the lady my name and phone number in case she did see Nana Lucy after I'd left. She wrote the information on her hand with a purple magic marker she found in her bag.

I rode the rest of the way down the street, past the

coulee and the cornfield that had brought back so many memories for Nana Lucy, then turned west and rode for a few more blocks. All the while, I scanned the area with my eyes, looking for a tiny, lost-looking old lady and possibly also a purebred brown dog.

By the time I turned back into the driveway, I was moving beyond concerned, into scared. I barely had time to think what to do next, however, before Scooby came racing around the side of the house to greet me.

"Scooby!" I cried, dropping Michael's bike on the grass as he threw himself at me. "Where have you been, you rat?! Where's Nana Lucy?"

"Leave them alone and they'll come home," Mrs. Forrest called from her yard. She was on her knees at the edge of her garden, pulling weeds. "He came running up to say hello to me not five minutes after you left."

Scooby jumped and slobbered all over me, but remained tight-lipped about his and Nana Lucy's earlier whereabouts. "Did you have a nice walk, Scooby?" I asked him. "Or did you wear Nana out?" As happy as I was to see Scooby, I was eager to get in the house and give Nana Lucy a piece of my mind about going out without telling me. I was so relieved, however, that it would be hard to be very stern with her. Mostly, I wanted to give her bony frame a big hug.

I attached Scooby to his chain, so I wouldn't have to worry about him, and went inside to find Nana Lucy.

"Nana? I have a bone to pick with you." My words were left hanging in the air. *Of course*, I thought, *she's probably worn out from their walk. I'll bet she's lying down.*

Nana wasn't resting on the sofa, however, nor was she dozing on the bed in my room. I checked Mom and Dad's bedroom, then Rachel's, my heart sinking. Was it possible that Scooby had just come back without Nana? Could I be sure they'd even been together in the first place?

Now I *really* was worried. I chewed my thumbnail, trying to think what to do. I needed a way to look for Nana Lucy fast; the early sun was climbing higher in the sky and it promised to turn into another hot, dry North Dakota day. I figured it wouldn't take long for Nana Lucy to become dehydrated, or overcome by the heat. And what if she became disoriented, or thought someone was chasing her?

I picked up the phone book and looked up Jace's number in the listings. A young boy answered. "Hello," I said. "This is Lucy Kellogg. May I please speak to Jace?" It suddenly occurred to me that he might not even be home, but a minute later he came on the line.

"Lucy?" He sounded happy to hear from me. "What's up? I was going to call you later to talk about what time …"

"Nana Lucy's missing," I interrupted him. The situation was feeling more and more urgent, and I didn't want to waste any time on small talk.

"Missing?" he said. "What do you mean?"

"Missing as in lost. I've been out looking but…" I told him what had happened. "Even if she just took a walk, that wouldn't necessarily be good," I said. "She's gotten lost before. I felt better when I thought Scooby was with her at least, but Scooby came home and Nana Lucy didn't. I'm really worried about her."

My voice shook on the last words, and I felt a pressing tide of fear rising in my chest. What would Mom and Dad say if something terrible happened to Nana Lucy when I was supposed to be keeping an eye on her? And how would I ever live with myself? *How?*

"I'll be right over," Jace said, and hung up on me. I waited anxiously, pacing around the kitchen. A loose pile of kitchen utensils lay by the sink, and I carried them back and forth absently for a few minutes, intending to put them away. When I couldn't think where they belonged, I ended up putting them back on the counter where I'd found them.

I thought to turn on the television to see if there were any news reports about a confused old lady who'd turned up somewhere, but the midday news was all about the city council's debate over whether to replace the town water tower, so I shut it off after a few minutes. Thankfully, Jace arrived soon after that.

"Any sign of her?" he said hopefully when I opened the back door for him.

I shook my head, then burst into tears. Jace came the rest of the way inside and wrapped me in his arms. He smelled great, and if I hadn't been so upset, it would have been delicious, but under the circumstances I couldn't even enjoy it.

"We'll find her, Lucy," he said, rubbing my back as I cried. "I promise."

I pulled away, not even caring what he thought of my tear-stained face and hair that I hadn't even had time to comb yet. "She's got Alzheimer's," I reminded him.

"Sometimes people like that wander away and no one finds them until they're … they're …" A fresh wave of tears made me unable to continue.

"No," Jace said, shaking his head adamantly. "Don't even think like that. We'll find her." He reached across me to where Mom kept a box of Kleenex on top of the fridge. "Here, blow your nose and let's go. There's no sense wasting any time."

I took the Kleenex and blew my nose obediently, then wiped the tears from my cheeks and took a deep breath. "All right." Hearing Jace sound so certain that we'd find Nana Lucy made me hopeful he was right. "Did you bring Bonnie?"

"Of course," he said. "And don't worry; she's like a bloodhound."

I smiled half-heartedly and followed him out to the curb where Bonnie was waiting. He opened the passenger door for me, then ran around to the driver's side and hopped in. "Let's hit the road." He turned the key.

Bonnie's engine revved, as if she were eager to help in the search for Nana Lucy. A second later, though, she gave a raspy cough, then hitched half-heartedly … and died.

"Unbelievable!" Jace hollered, pounding the heels of his hands on the steering wheel. "I can't believe she decided to conk out on me *now*. I thought she'd make it for at least a couple more months, if I babied her …"

I didn't say anything, just watched as he climbed out of the car and lifted the hood. I couldn't see him, but could hear him muttering and cursing as he poked around trying to find the source of the problem. Inside, my head was whirling with anxiety; without Bonnie, how would we be able to get around quickly enough to find Nana Lucy before something bad happened? I was getting close to the point where I knew I'd have to make a call either to Mom or to the Williston Police Department. I wasn't looking forward to doing either one.

Finally I leaned out the open window. "Maybe we could ask someone else for a ride?" I'd been thinking of Mrs. Forrest, but when I looked across the yard I saw that the Forrest car was no longer in the driveway.

Jace slammed Bonnie's hood closed and came around to where I was getting out of the car. "My parents are both at work," he said, shaking his head in discouragement. "The only one home at my house is my cousin, Jonah, and he's only twelve. Can you think of anyone else?"

I considered. "Well...actually, yes." I opened the car door and climbed out, heading towards the house with Jace following along behind. Scooby, who had been lying on the ground watching us, thought we were coming to see him and began jumping around wildly at the end of his chain. He'd have to wait until later, however; we had to find Nana Lucy before it got any hotter out. As it was, Scooby's tongue was hanging out and he was panting in the heat.

"Um, could you give him some water?" I asked Jace, pointing to Scooby's empty dish. "The hose is over there."

"Sure." Jace got busy taking care of Scooby, and I went inside.

The kitchen phone was heavy and reassuringly cool in my hand, but it still took me a minute before I got up the nerve to punch in the number. A glance at the clock told me it was noon; cheerleading practice should be over. After three rings, a chilly voice on the other end said, "Hollister residence."

"Sukie?" I whispered, suddenly short of breath, "It's me…Lucy. Don't hang up. I really need your help."

There was a pause before she answered, but when she did, her voice wasn't as cold, at least. "What's the matter? Did something happen?"

"It's Nana Lucy," I told her, starting to cry again. My words came flooding out. "My parents are out of town, and I'm supposed to be watching her, but when I got up this morning, she was gone. She's been missing for almost two hours and I can't find her anywhere. I'm really worried because it's getting so hot out, and she could be anywhere, and she's…"

"I'll be right over," Sukie said. "I'll watch for her on my way."

"Okay," I said gratefully. "Thanks." We hung up before I realized I hadn't even thought to warn her that Jace was here with me, but at that point I was beyond caring. I hoped Sukie was, too.

Outside, Jace was sitting on the steps petting Scooby, who was leaning up against him as if they were old friends. "I called Sukie," I told him. "She has a car, and she said she'd be right over."

Jace raised his eyebrows. "Oh…should I go?" he asked carefully. "I mean, I want to help you look for your grandma, but I don't want to make this situation any worse than it already is."

I shook my head. "No, I want you to help us look. Besides, three pairs of eyes are better than two."

A few minutes later, Olive came wheeling around the corner and pulled up into the driveway. I saw Sukie hesitate a moment when she saw Jace sitting on the steps beside me, but then she squared her shoulders and got out of the car. I hoped she wouldn't somehow think this was another trick.

"I got here as fast as I could," she said calmly as she approached. "No sign of Nana Lucy on the way."

Jace got to his feet and took a step towards Sukie. "Hi," he said. "Listen..."

Sukie held up her hand. "Save it," she said. "If you have something to say, we can talk about it after we find Lucy's grandma."

For once I appreciated Sukie's straightforwardness. I didn't want to waste any time straightening out a two-year-old mess while Nana Lucy was out there somewhere under the relentless sun that was now high in the sky.

"Okay," Jace agreed, and they both turned and looked at me as if waiting for direction. I was too freaked out to give any, however, so Sukie took charge. "Where have you looked so far?" she asked.

I quickly described the route I'd taken earlier on my bicycle, and added that I'd searched the house thoroughly not once, but twice.

"Is there any place in town that she likes to go?" Sukie asked, thinking. "Someplace she'd head towards?"

I shook my head. "She never really goes anywhere alone; one of us is always with her. I don't even know if she knows where things are without someone else driving. And the real problem," I added, "is that she doesn't always know where she is. She could take off for someplace thinking she's in Minneapolis, or even somewhere else she used to live."

Sukie looked serious. "Have you thought about calling the police?"

"I've thought about it," I admitted. "I'm just worried that…"

Jace interrupted. "I don't think the police really get involved unless a person's been missing for more than a couple hours."

"I would think that in a case like this, with an old person who's confused, they might not wait that long," Sukie countered. She sounded so certain that I immediately knew she was right.

"I-I just don't really want this situation to get blown up too big if we could find Nana Lucy ourselves," I said, feeling selfish for worrying about how much trouble I was going to be in already. And besides, if we called the police they'd come over and ask a lot of questions, which would take a lot of time, and all the while Nana would be out there getting more and more dehydrated. I shielded my eyes and squinted up towards the sun, which seemed unusually hot for June. Even just standing in the front yard, I could feel perspiration gathering between my shoulder blades and trickling down my back.

"Let's take another spin around the neighborhood, first of all," Sukie proposed.

Jace nodded. "Maybe I should stay here in case she

comes back while you're gone," he said. "Or in case some-one finds her and calls."

"That's a great idea," Sukie agreed, although I wasn't entirely confident that Nana would remember the number to call. "Lucy and I will drive around and see if we can spot her."

She looked at me, her gray eyes soft. "But if we can't find her in the next half hour or so, I think we should get the police involved. Okay, Lucy? We just can't take the chance of letting her be gone too long, especially on a hot day like this. It might be a bigger problem than we can handle."

I knew she was right. "Okay," I agreed miserably. "Let's go."

Jace stood on the steps and watched as we left; as Sukie backed Olive onto the street, he raised one hand and waved at me, his face worried.

"Thanks for doing this, Sukie," I said as soon as we were heading down the street. "I-I'm sorry about all the stuff that's happened."

Sukie shifted the car into second gear and kept her eyes on the road. "Yeah," she said noncommittally. "Well, maybe I've been overreacting a little. I mean … well, my dad says you told him there was some kind of misunder-standing or something. I don't really see how, but … hey!" She pointed towards a house we were passing on the right side of the street. "That's not her, is it? I left the house so fast I forgot to put my contacts in."

I peered eagerly out the passenger window, but shook

my head when I saw an unfamiliar lady around Nana's age rocking in her porch swing. "No, not her."

We continued down the street, scanning the sidewalks, lawns, and porches to no avail. Nana Lucy seemed to have eloped from the vicinity entirely. "Oh my God, Sukie," I moaned, "what if we can't find her? Or what if we do and she's hurt, or sick, or ..." I couldn't bring myself to think the worst.

"Relax," Sukie said calmly, downshifting so she could turn the corner. "If we can't find her, we'll just have to get more people to help. We've got plenty of time, and really, how far could she have gotten?"

I didn't say it out loud, but one thing that worried me was that I had no idea when Nana Lucy had even left the house. I'd slept so soundly that she could have climbed out of bed before dawn, and I wouldn't have known it.

We rode up one street and down another, asking anybody we saw if they'd seen an old lady who looked lost. "No," the answer inevitably came back. "Sorry." As the search went on, my heart grew heavier and heavier. Eventually, there was nothing to do but accept the fact that we'd come up empty-handed.

"Sukie," I finally said, "we're not going to find her. We've got to call the police."

Sukie must have been waiting for me to reach this conclusion, because she was pulling Olive around to head back to my house before I'd even finished the sentence. It wasn't long before we were pulling into my driveway again.

"No sign of her," she called to Jace, who had risen from the steps, looking hopeful, when he saw us pull up.

"We didn't even talk to anyone who'd seen her," I mourned. Sukie put her arm around me as we walked up the driveway towards the house, and I leaned against her gratefully. I'd only been up for a few hours, but it already felt like an entire day had passed and I knew there could be many stressful hours ahead.

Jace followed us into the house. "I can't believe this," I muttered over and over. "Where would she have gone?"

"I don't know, Lucy, I wish I did." I noticed that this time he didn't add any reassurance that we'd find her.

I sank down onto the couch. "We have to call the police."

Jace nodded, and exchanged a look with Sukie, who nodded too. "Let's go out to the kitchen," she suggested. "We can have something to drink and then you can make the call."

Numbly, I got up to follow them to the kitchen and sank into the chair Sukie'd pulled out for me. Jace sat down too, while Sukie pulled open the cupboard and took out three glasses. After spending seven years at our house, she didn't have to ask where we kept them.

She went to the refrigerator and peered in. "What does everyone want?" she asked. "Just water?"

"There's lemonade mix in the cupboard next to the microwave," I told her glumly.

Sukie found the container of mix and traced her finger down the side, looking for the instructions. "Stir three scoops of lemonade mix and one cup of sugar into two quarts of water," she read aloud. Turning on the kitchen faucet to let the water get cold, she looked around. "What should I make it in?"

"Just use the pitcher on the ..." I began, then stopped in mid-sentence. The pitcher next to the sink, which usually held the spatulas, whisks, and other kitchen utensils, was gone. Someone had dumped it out and left everything lying there, loose.

I'd seen the mess earlier, but I'd been too distracted by worry to put it all together. Now, it occurred to me that the only person who might have emptied the pitcher was ... my mind flew from the pitcher to the stream of cold water running from the faucet into the sink.

"I know where she went!" I cried, springing to my feet. "I know where we should look for Nana Lucy!" Not bothering to check whether Jace and Sukie were following me or not, I ran out the door.

thirty-two

"Head down towards the park," I instructed Sukie as we backed onto the street again. Jace was in the back seat and I was riding shotgun, my heart attempting to pound its way out of my chest.

"Where do you think she is?" Jace asked. "You seem so sure of where we're going."

I nodded. "One day Nana Lucy told me a story about when she was a little girl," I told them. "Her mother used to send her out to the fields with a pitcher of cold water for her father and brothers. She said she had to carry it carefully and slowly so that she wouldn't spill it all by the time she got there, because she knew how important that water was to them on a hot day."

"Well, it's certainly plenty hot today," Jace agreed, then looked guilty when both Sukie and I shot him a look.

Sukie was catching on, though. "So you think she got up this morning and thought that she needed to take water out to the fields."

I nodded, excited. "When you asked about the pitcher,

I realized it was missing. I didn't put it together earlier, but all of a sudden, it made sense."

We were getting close to the park, and I pointed. "Over there," I said. "That field reminded Nana of the one she used to cut through to bring the water."

Sukie pulled Olive up to the curb and we jumped out. "Nana Lucy!" I shouted. "Where are you?"

"Nana Lucy! Nana Lucy!" echoed Jace and Sukie. The three of us stood on the edge of the field; the corn crop had grown much higher since I'd been here with Nana the first time, and it was no longer possible to see across the top of it. We all listened intently, but the only thing we heard was the whispering of the corn stalks as they shifted and swayed in the hot summer air.

"I don't hear anything, do you?" Sukie asked us both.

Jace shook his head. "We're going to have to go into the corn," he said, "but we should stay in sight of each other. Otherwise we might miss something. Or get lost ourselves."

I took a deep breath. The idea of wading into the field of corn didn't appeal to me. The wall of stalks in front of us looked almost solid, but when we got closer I could see that there was enough space between the rows for a person to walk.

"Follow me," Jace said, leading the way into the corn. "Lucy, you walk down that row." He pointed to a row a few over from where he was, then indicated another one a few rows away on his other side. "Sukie, why don't you walk in that one?"

For some reason, I half expected Sukie to argue, but

she didn't. Instead, she stepped through the corn to where Jace had indicated. "Okay," was all she said. "Let's go."

Jace turned back to look at me, and our eyes met. "How are you doing?" he asked, reaching through the corn to take my hand. He gave it a gentle squeeze.

"Okay," I said, squeezing back and feeling stronger at the possibility that we might really locate Nana. "I just want to find her."

"Then let's do it."

The sun overhead was hot on the top of my head, but it would have been pleasant in the corn under different circumstances. The shifting stalks created a soft breeze, and the air seemed cooler than it had when we were standing on the edge of the field. If I was right about Nana Lucy being out in this field, at least she wasn't as exposed as I'd feared. Plus, I reminded myself, hopefully she had an entire pitcher of water with her if she got thirsty.

"Nana Lucy!" I called, "Where are you?"

"Yell if you can hear us!" Jace shouted. Again and again we called for her, with Sukie joining in as we waded deeper and deeper into the cornfield. Suddenly Jace held up his hand.

"What was that? I thought I heard something."

We froze, listening. "Hellooo…" came a faint, quavering call from somewhere off to our right.

"That's definitely Nana Lucy!" I cried, filled with joy that we were actually going to find her. Now if only she was all right. Jace and I grinned at each other through the rows of corn stalks between us, and I could hear Sukie murmuring excitedly on his other side.

"Yell again," Jace advised me. "Sukie and I will listen and try and get a better sense where she's at."

I obliged. "Nana Lucy!" I hollered. "Where are you?"

"I'm over here, dear," the voice came back faintly across the corn. "Where are you?"

"Stay where you are," Jace called to her. "We'll come to you."

Sukie pointed us in the direction the voice seemed to have come from, and we followed her across several more rows of corn. Still, no sign of Nana Lucy.

"Nana Banana," I yelled. "Nana Banana!" I was so relieved we were on the verge of finding her that I felt like crying with joy.

We listened for a response, but none came except for the sound of cornstalks shifting in the sudden light breeze. My happiness faltered, uncertain; that *had* been Nana Lucy's voice we'd heard, hadn't it?

Wordlessly, Sukie, Jace, and I moved forward through the corn, and suddenly there was Nana Lucy, sitting awkwardly on the ground. Her face was streaked with dirt and sweat, but a half-empty pitcher of water was settled safely in the loamy soil beside her.

"Why, hello," Nana Lucy said. "You can't imagine how glad I am to see you."

I fell to my knees beside her, holding back tears. "Nana," I exclaimed, "I've been so worried about you! Why did you leave without telling anyone?"

"Without telling anyone?" Nana Lucy repeated, looking perplexed. "Whatever do you mean? Mother sent me to bring water to Father and the boys, but I've forgotten what field they're in today. I walked all morning and still haven't found them. It must be afternoon by now!" Beneath the layer of field dust, my grandmother looked cross and tired.

"Oh, Nana," I sighed, looking up at Jace and Sukie. They were watching us, Sukie biting her lip.

"And now I've twisted my ankle," Nana added. "I've got to get this water to them or Father will be so dry and unhappy." She reached over and lifted the pitcher of water, her thin arm shaking under the weight. She held it out to Jace. "You look young and strong," she said. "Perhaps you could take it to them."

Jace was reaching for the pitcher cooperatively, but I couldn't help myself. "Nana," I told her, "you're mixed up. Your parents are dead; they died a long time ago. Don't you remember?"

Nana looked confused, then her eyes filled with tears. "My parents died?" she repeated. "But, I just saw them this morning..."

I realized too late that I should have used the reminiscence technique that Mom had told me about. "I-I...well, yes," I said, knowing it was probably too late to fix things now. "They died a long time ago, before I was even born. I'm Lucy, remember?" I finished miserably. "You're not a young girl, you're my grandmother."

Nana blinked her wet eyes and wrinkled her forehead. "Your grandmother," she said. "You're named after me." Then she nodded, her expression clearing. "Of course you are. I-I don't know what I was thinking." She looked around her. "And I came out here because…the cornfield…I thought they needed water." Her voice trailed off.

Now Jace did take the pitcher from her. "Why don't you let me carry that, Mrs. Kellogg," he said. "And maybe you can lean on Lucy; we should probably keep you off that ankle."

"Yes," agreed Nana faintly. Without another word, she let me put an arm around her waist and half-carry her feather-light form behind Sukie, who walked ahead of us, pushing the corn aside so we could find our way out of the cornfield.

"I'm so glad you came along," Nana Lucy whispered to me as we neared the edge of the field. "I wasn't sure how I was going to make it another step."

I smiled my gratitude at Jace as Sukie and I helped Nana Lucy the rest of the way to where Olive was waiting. "Nana, I think we'd better swing by the hospital and have the doctor take a look at that ankle," I suggested cheerfully. When we came out of the corn, I noticed that the ankle was swelling, and its purplish color was disturbing. I hoped it wasn't broken, but I wasn't taking any more chances where Nana Lucy was concerned.

"The two of you better squeeze into the back," Sukie advised Jace and me as we approached the car, and I realized she was right. Nana Lucy couldn't get into Olive's narrow back seat, especially with an injured ankle. I crawled into the back seat and Jace climbed in after me. Sukie pushed the passenger seat back into place and helped Nana Lucy get settled in front.

After she'd closed the door and was heading around

to the driver's side, Jace reached over and again took my hand in his. "I told you we'd find her," he whispered, smiling. His face and clothes were dusty from the corn, but his smile still made my stomach flip over.

I grinned back at him. "Yep," I said as Sukie opened the driver's door and got inside. "You did."

Sukie settled into her seat and reached for her seat belt. Buckling it, she peered back at us in the rearview mirror. "So," she said to Jace, "did Lucy tell you we used to call you 'He Who Shall Not Be Named'?"

Jace laughed. "Yes," he admitted. "I think she did say something about it, now that you bring it up."

"Yeah," Sukie said. "It was kind of stupid."

Jace considered. "Maybe now you could call me 'He Who Walks Among the Corn.'"

Sukie chuckled. "And I could be 'She Who Drives the Rescue Vehicle.'"

"Then I'm 'She Who Loves Her Friends,'" I told them, not joking at all.

Nana Lucy had twisted in her seat to look back at us, her face amused but confused. "I must say, you kids have lost me," she admonished.

"No way, Nana," I assured her. "That will never be the case, not *ever again*."

The Starbucks at Pike Place Market.

May 12th

Dear Lucy
    I'm having great fun on the "Savor Seattle" tour; today we visited Pike Place Market and ate lunch down by the wharf. The waiter dumped an enormous pot of steamed corn and crab legs right onto the table! We ate with our hands, but ended up requesting silverware; dentures and corn on the cob do NOT mix!
    Tomorrow it's the Space Needle. Remember this: I love you!
    Nana Lucy

LOND

PICCADILLY CIRCUS

thirty-three

When we got to the ER, it turned out that Nana wasn't able to fill out the paperwork, and when I looked things over, I realized I didn't know a lot of the information the hospital needed. I was left with no choice; I borrowed Sukie's cell phone and called Mom.

"Oh my goodness, Lucy," Mom breathed when I'd explained what happened. "Thank heavens you found her." I could hear Dad in the background, asking what had happened. "Listen, we're almost back to town; just tell the receptionist that I'll fill out the forms when we get there."

"Okay." Part of me was a little worried that Dad would be angry that I'd let Nana Lucy get lost. "Make sure you tell Dad she's all right, okay?"

"I'll tell him."

I closed the phone and handed it back to Sukie. "Are they mad?" she asked sympathetically.

"More just upset," I sighed. "I was supposed to keep anything like this from happening."

"Oh, now, that's nonsense," Nana Lucy said from my

other side. In spite of the pain I imagined her ankle must be causing her, she'd remained remarkably lucid ever since we'd left the cornfield. "You can't be expected to watch me every minute like I'm a child."

I didn't bother to tell her that that was *exactly* what my parents had trusted me to do.

"I'll tell them what happened; I must have had a dream that seemed so real that when I woke up I just went ahead and acted on it. Don't they watch those Hallmark movies? This sort of thing happens all the time!" Nana lifted her hand and circled a finger around next to her head in a "cuckoo" motion, making us all laugh. "Hello?" she said. "Dementia?!"

It felt *so* good to laugh, and I was still giggling when I remembered to go tell the receptionist that my parents would be coming with the insurance information. That seemed to make her happy, and not three minutes later a cute male nurse was pushing a wheelchair towards us to transport Nana Lucy back to the exam room.

"Come with me, won't you Lucy?" she said when we were helping her into the chair. "I'd feel better if you were along."

"Of course," I assured her. I couldn't help but think how many times over the course of my lifetime she'd offered me reassurance when I was nervous about something. I hadn't thought far enough ahead to imagine a time when *I* would be the calm, assured one.

The nurse pushed Nana Lucy's chair and I followed behind as we headed down a short hallway to the second exam room. "I'll put you right in here," he told us. "Dr. Browning should be in shortly."

"Something tells me we're in for a lo-o-o-ong wait," Nana Lucy muttered as soon as the nurse had left, closing the door behind him. I had a sudden flashback to Vista Manor, and wondered whether George was there, still waiting for the bus.

"I don't know, Lucy," Nana continued, oblivious to my thoughts. "I'm trying to cope with this situation as best I can, but sometimes..." She leaned over to peer down at her ankle, which had swelled so big the skin was stretched and shiny.

"Yeah," I told her. "I-I would hate it. I'd be mad."

Nana considered this. "I *am* mad!" she concluded. "It was hard enough when Samuel died, but at least I thought I'd get to spend my golden years traveling with my friends and seeing things I'd never seen before. That's a big deal for a girl who grew up on a farm, you know."

I nodded. Even though I didn't live on a farm, I'd never been farther than the Grand Canyon and had half-way hoped that when I was grown up I could take some trips with Nana myself.

"Your grandfather and I always wanted to travel but the store kept us tied down; we'd planned to see the world after we retired, but he kept putting it off, and well, look what happened." She got a faraway look in her eyes. "There was so much more I wanted to see. And now..."

I reached out and put my hand on her knee; it felt fragile and bony under her summer dress. "I'm sorry, Nana."

Nana Lucy looked down at my hand, then covered it

with her own. "Look at us," she said. "Just when you're growing into an adult, I'm heading the other direction, becoming a child. Who would have ever believed it?"

A lump sprang up in my throat that made it difficult to speak. "I don't know what to say," I squeaked. "But remember this: I love you so much, Nana."

Nana Lucy looked up, her cornflower blue eyes meeting mine. "I love you too," she said, giving a firm little nod as if to convince herself of her next words. "And that's one thing I'll never forget."

thirty-four

The doctor who examined Nana Lucy's ankle thought that it was badly sprained, but not broken. "It won't hurt anything to have an X-ray, however," he concluded.

"If you say so," Nana said with resignation.

The nurse returned and obediently wheeled Nana down the hall to X-ray.

"What exactly happened?" the doctor asked. He listened patiently as I explained.

"Well, she doesn't seem dehydrated, at least," he said once I'd finished.

"Of course not," I told him. "She had an entire pitcher of water along with her." I sighed, then admitted the worst. "My-my parents were out of town; I was supposed to be keeping an eye on her."

"Well, let's just focus on the fact that you found her, safe and sound," he said kindly. "And learn from this experience. People with Alzheimer's can become disoriented and wander off. As their memory problems worsen, events from the past may start to seem more vivid than the things that are happening in the present day."

I nodded, since that was just what had happened with Nana Lucy. She'd either remembered or had a dream about her mother telling her to bring water to her father and brothers in the field on a hot summer morning, and she'd headed off to do as she was asked. "I'm just glad she's okay," I told him. "And I will never let her out of my sight again."

"I know you won't. You never meant for this to happen, obviously."

The X-ray showed no evidence of a fracture, so the doctor wrapped Nana Lucy's ankle in a stretchy Ace bandage. "You'll want to put some ice on that as soon as you get home," he advised. "Try to stick to over-the-counter pain medication unless things get really painful." He wrote out a prescription. "If there's a lot of pain, you can fill this. And of course, stay off of it for at least a few days until the swelling goes down."

"I'll make sure she does," I promised. The nurse wheeled Nana Lucy back towards the waiting room where we found Mom, Dad, and Rachel waiting for us along with Jace and Sukie.

"Sukie told us everything," Mom said, getting up to hug me and then Nana Lucy. I shot Sukie a look of gratitude and she nodded in understanding.

"Mother, we're very glad you're all right," Dad said. "I don't know what we would have done if things hadn't turned out like this."

I didn't dare look at Dad, but I felt the lump returning to my throat. A moment later, however, I felt his hand on my shoulder. "Sounds like you did all the right things, Lucy."

I was too choked up to respond.

"She really did," Jace said, coming to my rescue. He gestured to himself and Sukie. "Lucy called in reinforcements as soon as she realized she couldn't find her grandmother, and if we hadn't found her when we did she was going to call the police."

Nana Lucy was listening to this from her seat in the wheelchair. "Lucy and her friends probably saved my life," she said, her expression grim. "I can't imagine what would have happened to me if I'd stayed in that field the rest of the day. And night," she added, shaking her head. "Bruce," she began, then hesitated. "Well, I guess this isn't the place to discuss it, but when we get home … well, I'm afraid maybe it isn't safe for me to stay at your house anymore."

"Mother," Dad began, "I'm sorry, but we've already talked about it not being safe for you to return to your apartment…"

"That's not what I'm saying," Nana interrupted. She took a deep breath, and looked around at all of us standing there. "Let's … let's just talk about it when we get home."

Dad nodded. The receptionist called to Mom to come and fill out some additional paperwork. I turned to Jace and Sukie, who were standing off to the side, waiting.

"You guys could probably go," I told them. "I should ride home with my family."

Sukie nodded. "I guess I can drop you at your house," she said gruffly to Jace.

Instantly I was sorry about the awkward situation I'd

put them in. "Oh, wait," I burst out. "Maybe I could ride along with you ..."

Jace held up his hand. "No, that's okay," he said, looking at me significantly. "There are some things I need to talk to Sukie about. I really want to talk to her alone about it."

I looked at Sukie, whose face had grown pink. "Is that okay with you, Suke?" I asked hopefully. I had a feeling that maybe Jace could accomplish what I hadn't been able to. And that maybe he was the one who *needed* to explain.

"Yeah," she said finally. "I guess so."

"Thank you. Both." I hugged Sukie, then Jace. "I don't know what I would have done without the two of you."

"No kidding," Sukie agreed, smiling in spite of the fact that her cheeks were still flushed.

"We're the best," Jace added with a grin. "You're one lucky gal."

Note to self: I couldn't agree more.

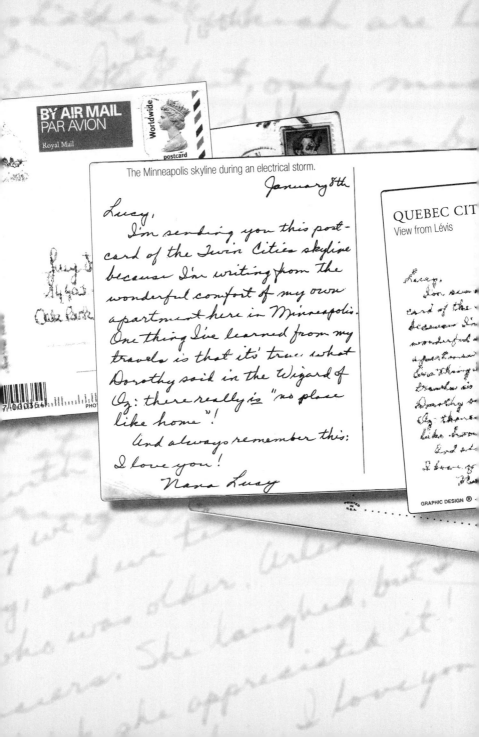

The Minneapolis skyline during an electrical storm.

January 8th

Lucy,

I'm sending you this postcard of the Twin Cities skyline
because I'm writing from the
wonderful comfort of my own
apartment here in Minneapolis.
One thing I've learned from my
travels is that it's true what
Dorothy said in the Wizard of
Oz: there really is "no place
like home"!

And always remember this:
I love you!

Nana Lucy

QUEBEC CIT
View from Lévis

Lucy,

GRAPHIC DESIGN ®

thirty-five

"So you're sure you have to work tonight?" Jace asked a few months later as we pulled up outside my house. "I was hoping we could catch a movie."

We were sitting in Jace's new pickup, Ozzie, and I inhaled the pine-tree smell of the air freshener he'd hung from the rearview mirror. "Sorry," I told him. "Nana's expecting me."

When the summer ended, I'd said goodbye to the AO and taken a job as an aide at Vista Manor, the dementia care facility where Nana Lucy was living. It was weird having Nana Lucy living in town but not at our house, and I felt better knowing that I could see her and know what was going on in her life almost every day.

Now I leaned across the seat to give Jace a kiss goodbye. "We'll do it next weekend," I promised. "I get off at nine, but I want to stay until I know Nana's gone to sleep."

"We can't do it next weekend. It's Cherilyn and Frank's wedding, remember?"

"Oh, yeah ... I can't believe I forgot."

Jace sighed. "All right. Maybe I'll call Nick and see what he's doing."

"Uh, I think Sukie said he was coming to watch her cheer tonight." Sukie had been dating one of Jace's friends, Nick Thompson, for the past few weeks, and so far things seemed to be going well. "We play the Saints, remember?"

"Crap."

"Okay, buck up," I told him. "You like football. Why don't you call Nick and see if he wants company?"

"Yeah. Maybe."

"Just don't go checking out any of the cheerleaders," I warned. "You already have a girlfriend, remember?"

"No way I could forget *that*, I assure you." He leaned across the seat to kiss me again; his familiar touch still made my stomach flip over.

I grinned against his lips. "Well, don't."

Fortunately, whatever explanation Jace had offered Sukie the day Nana Lucy got lost had been acceptable to her, and she now seemed to completely accept the fact that Jace and I were dating. Sukie and I had reestablished our friendship, but something about it still didn't feel quite the same. Maybe it was because during the weeks we'd been at odds, Sukie had become a real part of the cheer team; she was now as likely to call Fiona Barrett as she was to call me, and she'd even mentioned that she'd talked to Sarah Kenwood about the text message situation. Sarah had admitted she'd been the one who sent them, and apologized. Apparently Sukie had forgiven her, because I knew she was planning to go skiing in Montana with Sarah and her family over Christmas break.

"So," Jace was saying. "What kind of exciting activities do you have planned for the old folks tonight?"

"I thought we'd have a sock-matching party," I told him, grinning at how absurd it sounded. The truth was, sock-matching was one of the most popular activities among the female residents of Vista Manor. The men seemed to prefer more masculine pastimes, such as sorting nuts and bolts into bins. Jace got a kick out of the things we did, but I could tell he was genuinely interested because he always wanted to hear about it.

I didn't mind. I loved talking about Vista Manor, because it was one of my favorite places to be. Lately I'd even been thinking about going to med school someday, and eventually specializing in geriatric medicine. Or maybe I'd go into medical research and be the one who finally found a cure for Alzheimer's . . . who knew?

"I'd better fly," I told him, offering my face for one last kiss. "I told Rachel I'd give her a ride to her friend Lizzie's house before work."

That was the other big news; Mom and Dad had surprised me with an actual car. It was Mom's funny old Honda, which was fine by me; she'd bought herself a brand new Saab. I named the car Madge, which fit her perfectly. Madge got me everywhere I needed to go, and I knew we'd be together for the rest of the time I was in high school.

An hour later, I'd dropped Rachel off and arrived at Vista Manor wearing my work clothes. No more ruffled skirts and blouses for me; aides at Vista Manor wore baby blue scrubs. At least they were comfortable and easily identifiable to the residents, who know that blue scrubs equaled "someone who could help."

"Hey, Luce," called Vickie, the head RN, when she saw me letting myself onto the unit. "How's it going?"

"Great," I told her. "How's Nana today?"

Vickie considered. "Pretty good, I think. She seems to be developing a friendship with Dimitrius."

"Really?" I hoped it was just a friendship, but in truth, romantic attachments weren't unusual at Vista Manor. With so much white hair and glasses, it wasn't uncommon for residents with dementia to mistake other residents for someone they knew, and sometimes even their spouses. Actually, now that I thought about it, Dimitrius reminded even me of my grandfather, Samuel Kellogg. I could kind of understand what Nana might see in him.

"Avery's having a tough day," Vickie informed me. "Ever since he got up this morning, he's been convinced that his glasses are missing. We keep showing them to him but he swears they aren't his. And Gladdie has another urinary tract infection, so we have to watch her to make sure she doesn't fall." Urinary tract infections tended to make residents more confused and unsteady, I'd learned.

Vickie wasn't done yet. "Also, Victor refused his medication again, so he's a little owly."

"Okay, okay." I held up my hands in surrender. "So basically, same story, different day."

Vickie smiled. "Basically."

"I'm early, so I think I'll go say hi to Nana Lucy before I punch in," I told her.

"Sounds good. I'm sure she'll be happy to see you."

Nana Lucy was always happy to see me, but I wasn't sure anymore if it was because she was happy to see *me*, or just happy to have a visitor. Mom or Dad came up at least once a day, although Nana didn't always remember that they'd been there when I asked.

She was not in the main lounge area, nor in the dining room where a couple of the residents were helping Kjersten, another aide, wipe off tables after the evening meal. "Thank you, Mary, and you too, Dinah," Kjersten told them, winking at me. "I don't know what I would do without you two."

"It's always nice to have some help in the kitchen," Mary agreed.

I wandered away from the dining room and down the hall towards Nana Lucy's room. Beside each door hung a memory box, full of personal memorabilia that helped each resident identify their room. In Nana Lucy's box, Mom had placed a photo of Nana and Grandpa Sam as a young married couple, a postcard depicting the clothing store they'd run for years, and some pictures of Dad and Aunt Carol as children. She'd also included some of Nana's costume jewelry, and I'd donated the little snow globe Nana had sent me from Paris—the one with the Eiffel Tower inside.

I knew that the purpose of the memory box was to tap into very old memories, but I figured that visiting the Eiffel Tower wasn't something one easily forgot. Sure enough, Nana Lucy was never one of the residents who wandered around aimlessly, unable to find their room.

Still, it was undeniable that Nana Lucy was failing.

She'd had a brief period of calm after the day in the corn-field, but then suddenly started having stomach problems. When Mom took her to the doctor, he thought that the dementia medication might be causing it. This meant that there was no option but to let her dementia progress. Over the next several weeks, she'd really declined, which left my parents with no choice but to follow through on the wishes she'd expressed when we got home from the ER.

"Bruce," she'd said that day, settling onto the sofa and letting us prop her injured ankle up on a pillow, "you and Margo have been so good to let me stay here, and I've dearly loved spending this time with all of you. I'm no fool, however, so I want to be sensible about things. If this... disease is going to continue to get worse, it's not fair to you to have to watch me all the time to make sure I don't do anything silly or dangerous. I think, well, I think I'll have to move to someplace more secure. I know there's probably someplace like that nearby, and I'd really like to stay close if I could."

"Vista Manor," I'd whispered before I even knew the words had come out of my mouth.

Nana Lucy turned to look at me, then nodded firmly. "Vista Manor," she'd agreed. "Indeed."

Things had moved quickly, too quickly, after that, and before I knew it I had my bedroom all to myself. It meant more restful nights of sleep, of course, but for weeks I was the one crying into my pillow.

"Hi, Nana," I said now, when I found her sitting in her room, rocking away in the comfortable rocking chair Dad had brought from our living room. She often spent hours in that chair; the rhythmic rocking seemed to soothe her.

"Why, hello!" Nana greeted me pleasantly. "How lovely to have a visitor! And such a pretty one!"

Despite her disease, Nana's cheeks had color. But she'd been eating less, and seemed less interested in food. Even Oreos didn't tempt her the way they once had.

"It's me, Lucy," I told her, smiling. "Your grand-daughter. The grandest one of all." I no longer felt awkward identifying myself to Nana Lucy. Since starting work at Vista Manor, I'd learned a lot about dementia, and I knew that even though Nana was no longer the person she'd once been, it still helped both of us to make sure she felt comfortable and happy.

Nana nodded and smiled back at me, but didn't stop her rocking. Someone had started a CD in her player, and strains of classical music drifted softly in the background.

"Would you like me to brush your hair, Nana?" I'd discovered that having her hair brushed was something she enjoyed, and I was happy to do it for her whenever I got the chance.

"Why, yes," Nana Lucy said, stopping her chair mid-rock. "Please do. You girls are so good to me."

I picked up the brush that lay on top of her dresser and moved around behind her chair. "So," I said, gently pulling the brush through her fine cloud of hair. "I hear you've made a new friend."

"Yes," she said simply. I wasn't sure whether she knew what I meant or not. Either way, she was too distracted by the pleasure of having her hair brushed to elaborate.

I continued the gentle brushing, working my way through her hair until suddenly Nana Lucy's head lolled back against my hand. A moment later she began to snore gently. *Uh-oh*, I thought. I hadn't meant to put her to sleep, and I knew I couldn't leave her without worrying that she'd relax too much and tumble out of the chair.

Setting the brush down on the little table, I moved around the rocker and knelt beside it. "Nana?" I said softly. "If you'll wake up for a minute, I'll help you into bed."

She mumbled in response, but kept her eyes closed while I eased her out of the chair and onto the bed. Once she was settled, her lids lifted and she looked at me, her cornflower blue eyes as clear as I'd ever seen them. "Oh," she said. "My sweet Lucy."

As surprised tears filled my eyes, hers drifted closed again and her face grew slack with sleep. I managed a deep breath around the lump in my throat and pulled a blanket from the end of the bed, smoothing it gently over her and committing to memory what might just be the last time Nana Lucy would look at me with recognition.

"Nana," I whispered when she was tucked in snugly. "I'm glad you remembered me, even just for a minute. And I hope you also remember this: I love you more than you could know. You're the best grandmother I could ever have wished for. No matter what, I'll never forget *you*."

And with that, because I knew it was time, I let her go.

Information About Alzheimer's Disease

Alzheimer's disease is a progressive brain disorder that gradually destroys a person's ability to learn and remember, to use good judgment, to communicate, and to carry out basic daily activities. As Alzheimer's disease progresses, individuals may also experience changes in personality and behavior. Because of these changes, a person with Alzheimer's may forget your name, see things or hear things that aren't there, get lost, blame other people when they lose things, and do or say the same things over and over. These problems can cause them to become confused, frustrated, nervous, or even angry.

A 2007 study by the National Institute on Aging (NIA) found that there are now more than five million people in the United States living with Alzheimer's disease. Scientists still do not know what causes the disease or how to cure it, but new treatments are being explored, and there is already some progress in learning how to slow down the progression of the disease. Research has shown that even if someone in your family has Alzheimer's, this does not necessarily mean that you or your parents will ever develop it.

There are a lot of things that you can do to help care for someone with Alzheimer's disease. You can take walks with them, play familiar games, sing songs or listen to music, look at old photos, or put together a collection of things that help them remember special times from the past. Sometimes people with Alzheimer's find simple repetitive tasks, such as sorting items or folding towels, to be soothing.

Taking care of a family member with Alzheimer's is a very challenging and difficult job. Caregivers can easily become worn out, frustrated, impatient, or sad. If someone in your household has Alzheimer's, you may also find yourself feeling sad or angry at times. It is important to talk to someone about your feelings and to ask questions if you do not understand what is happening.

A good place to look for helpful information about Alzheimer's disease is at the Alzheimer's Association website, located at www.alz.org.

About the Author

Susan Thompson Underdahl is a North Dakota native who likes to believe she does not have any trace of a midwestern accent. She once had an eight-year friendship with a ghost, and she can occasionally breathe underwater, but not on command. During the weekdays, she is a neuropsychologist specializing in the evaluation and treatment of dementia and brain injury. On evenings and weekends, she is the keeper of one daughter, two sons, and three stepdaughters, in addition to two cats, two dogs, and one husband. On her lunch hours, she writes.

A conversation with
Susan Thompson Underdahl

1. *Tell me about what inspired this book. Did you draw on your own experience, as you did in* The Other Sister?

I'm fairly certain that every writer draws on his or her own experience in writing any book, and quite a lot of my life experiences found their way into *Remember This*. I grew up in Williston, North Dakota, where the story takes place, and I did, in fact, have a job as the hostess at the Adobe Oven restaurant. Much of what happens to Lucy at the AO actually took place in my own life; it was fun to think back to that time.

Another primary source of inspiration came from my present-day life, in which my "regular job" is as a clinical neuropsychologist, evaluating people with memory and other cognitive problems. In the course of my practice, I've met many, many Nana Lucys and their families, and have always been struck by the complex, devastating effects of Alzheimer's disease. The Kelloggs represent a typical family trying to support each other as one of them slowly slips away.

2. *It seems to me that your book is concerned with changes, good and bad, and how people deal with them—Nana Lucy is changing, Sukie and Lucy's relationship is changing, and ultimately Lucy's perception of herself is changing.*

Every single day brings changes, and it can be very frightening and frustrating to feel like we don't have control of what's happening. Even positive changes can be stressful in their own way. People respond differently: some fall apart, some lean on each other, some find strength they didn't know they had. I think that the most unexpected, challenging changes are often the ones that teach us about ourselves and force us to grow the most.

3. *Alzheimer's and other degenerative diseases that affect memory are becoming increasingly common as the population ages. Do you think this is having an impact on teenagers, as their Baby-Boom grandparents face these challenges? It seems to me that the dawn of independence for teens and the twilight of independence for the elderly coincide in interesting ways.*

Because of the aging population, it is likely that most of us will soon know, or know of, someone who has Alzheimer's disease. I feel, for that reason, that it's important to bring this health issues to the fore. In this book, young Lucy faces her grandmother's decline at the very time she is growing into her adult self. I wanted to show the contrast, that the young Lucy is finding out who she is while the elder version, Nana Lucy, is losing her own sense of self.

4. *The relationships Lucy and her mother have with Nana Lucy seem very different. Can you talk a little about that? Lots of teen books feature mother-daughter relationship issues, but I think including another generation adds something.*

Isn't it interesting how differently Lucy and her mother experience Nana Lucy? To young Lucy, her grandmother is a loving touchstone and source of unconditional support. For Margo Kellogg, her relationship with her mother-in-law often leaves her feeling inadequate and insecure. I think that our perception of how others see us is sometimes more a reflection of how we feel about ourselves. In the end, both Lucy and her mother realize the same thing: Nana Lucy is vulnerable and human, just as they are. Even through the terrible circumstances of an illness, the characters maintain a sense of humor and grow to understand each other better.

5. *You're also a doctor, with a full-time practice. How do you balance writing with your other work?*

It seems like there are never enough hours in the day, but I usually try to work on writing-related things over the noon hour. On a rare occasion, I'll take an entire day off work, go to the library, and try to focus on getting some writing done. Sometimes this works, and other times not; it feels like too much pressure. Two years ago I wrote a novel in nineteen days during the National Write a Novel in a Month festivities. I seem to write best on the fly; I'm simply not one of those writers who agonizes over every word and takes days to write a page. If the ideas are flowing, I might bang out an entire chapter over my lunch hour.

6. Can you talk a little about the challenges and rewards of writing YA?

I didn't set out intending to write young adult novels. In fact, when I wrote *The Other Sister* I wasn't thinking at all about the intended audience, simply that I had a story I wanted to tell. I quickly discovered, however, that I needed to educate myself on what teen life is like these days; my editor informed me that I was writing "very old-fashioned young adult novels." When I thought about this, it made perfect sense: the last young adult novel I'd read was back in the mid-1970s! He kindly gave me a "summer reading list" of contemporary YA books and I read them all, discovering that teen characters in novels today are much smarter and more self-aware than they used to be. I had to learn to dial up my characters a bit, both to make them believable and to appeal to readers, who are much more sophisticated than I was when I was a teen!

As far as the rewards, well, writing YA has given me a chance to meet so many great young readers, and to really feel like I'm impacting their lives the way my own was impacted by memorable books at their age.